TERRIFIC TALES

TERRIFIC TALES

Isabella Lewis

VALANCOURT BOOKS
CHICAGO

Terrific Tales by Isabella Lewis
Originally published in 1804
First Valancourt Books edition, November 2006

ISBN 0-9777841-5-0

Published by Valancourt Books
Chicago, Illinois
http://www.valancourtbooks.com

Lewis, Isabella.
 Terrific tales / Isabella Lewis. -- 1st Valancourt Books ed.
 p. cm.
 ISBN 0-9777841-5-0
 1. Apparitions. I. Title.
 BF1451.L6 2006
 133.1--dc22
 2006024233

Set in Bembo 11.5/14.5

Printed in the United States of America

A NOTE ON THE TEXT

THIS Valancourt Books edition of *Terrific Tales* is the second edition of this rare work. It was first published at London in 1804, printed by R. Cantwell of Temple Bar for J. F. Hughes of Cavendish Square. James Fletcher Hughes was an important publisher of Gothic fiction between 1800 and 1811, capitalizing on the successes of other publishers by issuing derivative works like T. J. Horsley Curties's *The Monk of Udolpho* (1807) and Edward Montague's *The Demon of Sicily* (1806). Hughes was a somewhat less than reputable publisher, and published books by "Mary Anne Radcliffe" and "Mrs. Edgeworth", both almost certainly pseudonyms, in order to capitalize on the successes of Ann Radcliffe and Maria Edgeworth.

Nothing at all is known of the author of the present work. Isabella Lewis never published another book, and the name may in fact be a pseudonym intended to evoke two of the most popular Gothic novelists of the period, Isabella Kelly and M. G. Lewis.

This edition reprints verbatim the text of the first edition, retaining inconsistent spellings and occasional poor grammar. A few very obvious printer's errors, such as "whloe" for "whole", "enentering" for "entering", the unnecessary duplication of words like "of" or "the", and occasional missing quotation mark, have been silently corrected.

TERRIFIC TALES.

BY

ISABELLA LEWIS.

" Black Spirits and White,
" Red Spirits and Grey,
" Mingle, Mingle, Mingle,
" You that mingle may."

Scale of Dragon, tooth of Wolf,
Witches mummy, maw and gulf.
MACBETH.

LONDON :
Printed by R. Cantwell, 33, Bell-Yard, Temple-Bar,
FOR J. F. HUGHES, NO. 5, WIGMORE-STREET,
CAVENDISH-SQUARE.

1804.

The Count of Macon, in the midst of life and health, transported into the air by a spectre in the shape of a horse.

The Count of Macon, a gentleman of very inordinate passions, exercised a species of tyranny against the ecclesiastics and their adherents without giving himself the least concern either to conceal or give colour to his excesses. He even made a boast of them, and practised them openly. One day being seated in his palace, accompanied by a numerous train of nobility and others, a stranger on horseback was seen to enter, who advanced towards him, and said, "that having something of importance to communicate, he desired that he would follow him." The Count arose, and having arrived at the door, found a horse waiting for him; he mounted, and was immediately conveyed into the air, exclaiming with an awful voice to those who were present, "assistance, for heaven's sake assistance." The whole town were alarmed and ran to his exclamations; however, they very soon lost sight of him, and had no doubt but the demon had carried him off with him to be a companion of his torments, as a punishment for his excessive passions.

Pierre, the venerable abbot of Cluni, relates this extraordinary fact happened in his days, and seen by the whole city of Macon, in his work intituled: *Petrus venerab. lib. 2, de miraculis, Chap. 1st. page* 1299.

Count Despilliers and one of his soldiers nearly smothered between the bed and mattrass by an invisible hand.

COUNT DESPILLIERS the elder, when young, and captain of the cuirassiers, took up his winter quarters in Flanders. One of his cavaliers came one day to beg of him to change his host, saying, "that every night a spectre haunted him in his room and prevented him sleeping." The Count dismissed his cavalier, and laughed at his simplicity. A few days after this, the same cavalier went to make him the same entreaty; when the captain irritated, would have discharged a volley of *coups de baton* at him, had he not with great agility left the room. At length he returned a third time to the charge, and protested to his captain that he could put up with it no longer, and should be obliged to desert, provided his quarters were not changed. Despilliers, who knew the cavalier to be a brave soldier and extremely sensible, said to him with an oath; "I will go and sleep in the same room with you to night, and see what it is."

About ten o'clock in the evening the captain went to the cavalier's lodging; and having put his pistols upon the table, laid down in his cloaths, in a bed without curtains, with his sword beside him. About twelve o'clock he heard something come into the room, turned the bed topsy-turvy, and enclosed the soldier and his captain under the mattrass and *paillasse*. Despilliers had the greatest trouble in the world to disengage himself to find his sword and pistols again, when he returned home with them agitated and confused. The Cavalier's quarters were changed the next day, where he slept tranquilly at the house of his new host.

Mr. Despilliers related this adventure to every body that wished to hear him; he was a man of undaunted courage, and had never known what it was to retreat. When he died he was field marshal to the armies of the Emperor Charles VI. and governor of the fortress of Segedin.

The body of a woman that had been hanged invested by the devil.

IT happened at Paris, on the 1st of January 1613, during those heavy falls of rain which at that period inundated the country, that a young gentleman of that city, who was returning home about four o'clock in the afternoon from the house of one of his friends with whom he had passed the major part of the day, he met in a little alley, a young lady very handsomely dressed (apparently some courtezan) in a robe of pinked taffety adorned with a pearl necklace, and several other brilliant and apparently rich jewels, who as if astonished, and yet with a smile upon her countenance addressed the gentleman, and said, "Although, Sir, this tempestuous weather does not suffer me to commit myself to its mercy, I would at all times rather be exposed to it, than for it to be said, that I am the least inconvenience in the world to any one; occupying here without any permission, the entrance to your lodging; but should it be a thing that I can do without incurring your displeasure, I shall be as much obliged to you for it as any one of those who have ever had the honor of being your most affectionate servants." The gentleman looking at her attentively, judging by the exterior, and observing the politeness with which she accosted him, thought it his duty to return it, as well by words as actions, consequently replied: "I am exceedingly sorry, Miss, that my arrival has been too tardy for you to be enabled to witness the service that I have at all times devoted to the ladies, and principally to those of your quality; in order to verify my assertion I not only make you the offer of my lodging, but of every thing that you think me empowered to bestow wherein I can render my most humble services, and in the mean time I beg you would take the trouble to walk in, until the rain is over." The young lady said to him: "I have never,

Sir, merited the offer you make me, but I will endeavour to return it in some instance or other when an opportunity shall present itself: however, I shall beg of you only to permit me to wait here the arrival of my carriage, for which I have just now sent my servant." "No," said the gentleman, "you will oblige me much to walk in and take part of a cold collation, till your carriage comes; and although you may not be received according to your quality and merit, I will endeavour to render you every accomodation in my power."

At length, after much altercation on both sides, the young lady consented, and appeared exceedingly vexed at her servants' not coming. The day passed over without the lackey's having legs, or the carriage wheels, to arrive. Supper time being come, the gentleman endeavoured to treat her in the handsomest manner he was able. When it drew near the hour for repose, the young lady intreated him, that since he had done her so much honor as to afford her an asylum, that he would in addition to his favours accommodate her with a single bed, hinting that it would not be becoming of a young lady to admit any one to partake of it; which he readily granted. While she was making preparations to pass the night alone, the gentleman presumed to display his gallantry in conversation, to which she replied in such bewitching language, that after a tedious parley between love and honour, the young hero was seduced. During the night he had a dream which tormented him exceedingly, respecting her who was sleeping by his side. The morning being come, he arose, and fearing lest any one should come and see him, and that finding the young lady, they might suppose something, he sent his servant to wake her; to whom she replied, "that she had had but very little sleep in the night, consequently begged that she might not be disturbed:" to which the servant made no reply, related that to his master, who after having made a few turns in the city, returned with some of his friends, but would not suffer them to go into his chamber until he had first sent his man to beg of the young lady to get up. After all he resolved to go himself in order to excuse himself to her for his inattentions; when on entering the room, he drew the curtains, and having called her by several endearing names, he went to take her by the arm, but he felt her as cold as marble, and without any pulse or breath whatever; on which account being terrified, he called his host, but in vain; for he being arrived accompanied by several others, they found her a lifeless corse. The justice and physicians were sent for, who with one accord said that it was the body of a woman who some time past had been hanged, and that it was a devil who had invested himself with her body in order to deceive that unfortunate gentleman.

They had scarcely uttered these words, but in the sight of all, a thick and obscure smoke arose in the bed, which lasted for a few moments, and with the most unpleasant odour; it clouded their senses in such a manner, that they lost sight, without knowing how she had escaped that was in bed; in fine, the vapour diminishing, by degrees totally disappeared; they only found the place where the carcase laid. Every one generally deplored the accident that had befallen the young gentleman, whom I leave you to suppose whether he was astonished in having reposed the whole night with a demon, and that the effect of a thing so miraculous and difficult to believe, should have happened in his apartment. Were it only through the testimony of those who have heard of it, and the evidence of those who were present, it would be sufficient to confirm it.

*The Ghost of Sancho three months after his death appearing to
Pierre d'Englebert in Spain, at his bed-side by moon-light.*

PIERRE D'ENGLEBERT being one night in his bed wide awake,
saw in his chamber, by the light of the moon, the spirit of a
man named Sancho, whom he had several years before sent
at his expence to the assistance of Alphonzo, King of
Arragon, who was carrying on the war in Castile. Sancho
returned from that expedition safe and sound. Some time
after, he fell sick and died at his own house.

Four months after his decease Sancho presented himself
to Pierre d'Englebert completely naked. He set about
uncovering the wood ashes which were still alight in the
fire-place, as if to warm himself, or in order to shew himself
more distinctly. Pierre asked him who he was. "I am,"
replied he, with a broken and hollow voice, "Sancho your
servant."—"And what are you come to do here?"—"I am
going," said he, "into Castile with several others, in order to
expiate the ill that we did during the last war, at the same
spot where it was committed. As to what more particularly
relates to me, I pillaged the ornaments of a Church, and I am
condemned on that account to undertake this journey. You
can much assist me by your good works; and my lady your
wife who is still indebted to me eight sous, being the residue
of my salary, will oblige me infinitely to give them to the
poor in my name."

Pierre asked him concerning a friend of his, one Pierre
de Fais, who was but recently dead. Sancho told him that he
was saved. "And Bernier our fellow-citizen, what has
become of him?"—"He is damned," said he, "for having
badly acquitted himself in his office as judge, and also for
having harassed and pillaged the widow and the
innocent."—Pierre added:—"Can you give me any

intelligence of Alphonzo, King of Arragon, who died some few years since?"—At that moment another spectre that Pierre had never seen before, and which he remarked distinctly by the light of the moon seated by the window, said:—"Do not ask him about the King Alphonzo, he cannot tell you; he has not been long enough with us to know any thing of him. As for me I have been dead these five years, I can inform you. Alphonzo has been with us some time; but the monks of Cluni have taken him from us: I do not know where he is now."—At the same time addressing himself to his companion Sancho:—"Come," said he, "let us follow our associates, it is time to depart."—Sancho reiterated his importunities to Pierre his lord, and left the house.

Pierre awoke his wife, who was sleeping by his side, and who had neither seen any thing nor heard any thing of this dialogue, and asked her: "Do not you owe any thing to Sancho our servant who died lately?"—"Yes, I owe him eight sous," replied she. At these words Pierre no longer doubted of the truth of what Sancho had told him; gave the eight sous to the poor, added to them many of his own, and ordered mass and numerous prayers to be put up for the soul of the deceased.

Pierre d'Engelbert, who after having lived a long time in that age, wherein he was reputed for valour and honor, retired after the death of his wife, in the order of Cluni, related this discourse in presence of the bishops of Oleron and Orman, in Spain, and several ecclesiastics, to Pierre, the venerable abbot of Cluni, who speaks of it in his work intituled, *Petrus venerab. abb. Cluniæ de miracul. lib.* 1, *chap.* 28, *p.* 1293.

The apparition of the Duke of Milan's brother to two merchants.

ABOUT the beginning of the 16th century as two Merchants of Milan were going to the fair of Lyons in France, they met upon mount Cenis, near a place vulgarly called the devil's bridge, on account of a continual wind which blows there, a man uncommonly tall who presented to them a letter, commanded them to return and commit that letter to his brother Lewis. Astonished at that commission, they asked him who he was. The spirit replied, "I am Galeas Sfortta,"— and disappeared.

The Merchants returned to Milan, and from thence to Vigevans, where the duke of Milan was at that time, and committed to him the letter; however, they were arrested, thrown in prison, and interrogated as to the fact. After having lain some time and always persisting in their innocence, and by whom they were ordered, they were set at liberty. A counsellor belonging to the Duke, named Vincent Galeas, took the letter which was written upon paper and folded as they usually fold letters in Italy, sealed with a very fine brass wire; its contents were as follows:

"Lewis, Lewis, take care of yourself, the French and Venetians are forming an alliance against you, in order to ruin you; but if you will furnish me with three thousand pistoles, I will endeavour to reconcile the spirits."—Adieu.

The superscription or signature was, "The spirit of thy brother Galeas."

Every one was surprized at this adventure. Some looked upon it as a jest, while others conceived it more advisable to make a deposit of the three thousand pistoles, in order to comply in some measure with the desire of Galeas; but the Duke refused listening to it, and thought that he should be laughed at if he consented.

The circumstance, however, proved true; for before the expiration of the year, duke Lewis was taken by the French and Venetians, who being leagued against him, made war and conducted him to France, where he died in prison.

Hobgoblins that appeared near the Castle of Lusignan in 1620.

ON Wednesday evening 22d of July 1620, there appeared between the castle of Lusignan and the park, seemingly upon the river, two men composed of fire extremely powerful in complete armor, with a flaming sword in one hand, and a burning lance in the other, who were attacking each other in the most vigorous combat; and being both armed with similar weapons, the contest lasted a considerable time; so that in the end one of the two who was wounded and falling gave such a horrible shriek that awoke several of the inhabitants of the high and low town. Soon after this battery was finished, a long train of fire seemed to pass along the river and penetrate into the park, followed by several fiery monsters similar to monkies. Several poor people who were in the forest picking up sticks met this prodigy, which nearly frightened them to death, and amongst others a poor labourer was so terrified, that it threw him into a dangerous fever which never left him. This was not all, for so were the soldiers alarmed with the shriek that they had heard, that they mounted upon the walls to see from whence the voice proceeded. There passed over their heads an amazing flock of birds, some black, others white, screaming with a hideous and uncommon noise, preceded by two flambeaux, and a figure resembling the complete form of a man followed them hooting like an owl. The people were so alarmed at this vision that they longed for the approach of day to relate their terrors.

Spectres that haunted the house of a Gentleman in Silesia through his rash wishes.

IN 1609 a gentleman residing in Silesia having invited several of his friends to dine with him, the hour of the sumptuous entertainment arrived. Seeing himself frustrated by the excuses of his guests, he entered his apartment in the greatest rage, and began exclaiming—"Since nobody will deign to visit me, may the devils participate my fete."—Saying which, he left his house, and went to church, where the curate was preaching. He listened a long time with the greatest attention. Whilst he was there, several men on horseback, exceedingly tall, and quite black, went into the gentleman's court-yard, met one of the servants, and commanded him to go and tell his master that his guests were come. The valet, greatly terrified, ran to the church to inform his master, who very much astonished, related it to the curate.

The latter finishing his sermon, advised him to order all his family out of the house. This was no sooner said than executed; but in consequence of the haste that they made in escaping from that awful abode, they left in one of the rooms a little child sleeping in a cradle. The guests, or to speak more properly the devils, began to overturn the tables, to howl, to look out of the windows in the shape of bears, wolves, cats, and hobgoblins, holding in their hands glasses of wine, fish, and boiled and roasted joints of meat. As the neighbours, the gentleman, the curate, and others, were contemplating the like spectacle with horror, the poor father began to exclaim, "Alas! where is my poor infant?" The last word was scarcely from his lips, when one of the black guests brought the child in his arms to the windows, and shewed him to all those who were in the street. The gentleman, quite distracted, addressed himself to his trusty servant—"My friend, what shall I do?"—"Sir," replied the young man trembling, "I will recommend my life to God, and then in his name I will enter the house, and in consideration of his favor and assistance, I will bring you away the child." "Well," said the master, "God accompany, assist, and fortify you." The servant having received the benediction of his master, the curate, and other gentlemen who were present, went home, and approaching the room where the dark guests were sitting, he prostrated himself upon, and recommended himself to, the Almighty; then opened the door, and beheld the spectres in a horrible form, some seated, others standing, others crawling upon the floor. They all of them darted towards him, and exclaimed together in a hollow voice—"What brings you here?"—The servant trembling with fear, at the same time emboldened by his trust in the Omnipotent, addressed himself to the mischievous one who was holding the infant, and said, "Here! deliver me that child." "I will not," replied the spectre, "it is mine; go and tell thy master to come for it himself."—The servant insisted, and said—"I am doing the office that God hath commanded me, and know all that I do conformable to that is acceptable to him. Being here in virtue of my office, in the name and assistance of his blessed Son, I snatch from thee and seize this child, which I shall carry to his father."—Saying this he caught hold of the infant, and clasped it closely in his arms. The black guests replied with the most dismal shrieks in these words—"Thou wretch, thou profligate, leave the child, or thou shalt perish."—But despising their threats, precipitated out of the house unhurt, and restored the child into the hands of his father. Some days after this the unwelcome visitors disappeared; when the gentleman returned home, and ever after lived as a true christian.

Spirit of a Gentleman which burst through a casement in his Daughter's bed-chamber, at the hour of his death, invisible to every one except a dog, who continued barking till it vanished.—A fact.

IN the year 1663, a private gentleman, married, rich, and of a good family, lived in the street des Ecoufles at Paris. His family consisted of his wife, and a son about five years old, who was the only one left of six other children that they had had together. The father of this lady was infirm, of an agreeable conversation, and visited them often. A little time before his decease he went to see them, and testified to the lady his daughter that he had just come to bid them adieu before his departure. She embraced him with affection; and calling her son who was playing in the garden with some other children, she told him to come and salute his grand-papa, and shew him his new cloaths that she had had just made for him. He appeared very much pleased at it, and kissing tenderly his grand-son, said: "My little dear, in a short time you shall have a prettier one than this, you shall wear a black one for grand-papa."—"Fie! fie! father," replied the lady; "why are you always speaking about that? Do not think of such gloomy subjects."—"Ah! daughter," replied the old gentleman, "I perceive it well, I am drawing near the verge of dissolution; but God's will be done; I will come and see you once more."—After these words he left the room, and set off the next day for his country-house at Crecy, where his affairs called him. Having arrived there, he found himself very ill; and as his situation was dangerous, a particular friend imparted the news to his son-in-law, and requested him to come with all possible speed. As soon as the letter was received, the gentleman sent for two post-horses, and left town immediately with his valet; so that they arrived at Crecy about four o'clock in the afternoon. They found the old gentleman approaching his last moments, but still sensible. They seized the opportunity to make him receive the sacrament. The patient grew worse; he went into convulsions, and died about eleven o'clock in the evening of the following day. The son-in-law undertook the care of inhuming the body, and gave orders for a handsome funeral. After that he had some affairs of the succession to regulate, which obliged him to defer for some time his return.

During his absence, his wife who was at Paris, and who loved as tenderly her dear father as she was beloved, and knew by the letter of advice the danger he was in, was inconsolable, and did nothing but weep: she was left with her son, her *femme de chambre,* and two other servants. As she was naturally fearful, she had a little bed made for her *femme de chambre* near her's, in order to dispel her glooms, and slept with her beloved son, whom she could never suffer to be a moment from her.

The *femme de chambre* on her side, in order to have a second, likewise put upon the foot of her bed the dog belonging to the house, to watch and be her protector. Order was so strictly observed that every one was in bed before ten in the evening.

It happened that the same day that their dear parent died, our faithful guardians after the greatest agitations, began scarcely to taste the sweets of a tranquil sleep, when about eleven at night they were awakened suddenly by a violent noise that was made at one of the windows of their chamber which looked into the garden. The casements and their shutters according to the ancient mode were divided into several pannels. Although the whole had been perfectly secured, a top pane and a part of the shutter opened half way without breaking, in a manner supernatural, and a rustling was heard similar to a person with a silk gown; and entering forcibly through the cavity. Judge how a prodigy so surprizing must have alarmed the mistress and her *femme de chambre*. Fear rendered them quite motionless, and deprived them of speech. The dog at the first noise that he had heard, precipitated off the bed, and ran barking from one end of the room to the other. He was so agitated that he struck his head against the walls and chairs with as little care as though he had been insensible of the blows. He continued that fatiguing trim till day-light, when being totally exhausted, he fell down with lassitude, couched upon the floor, and fell asleep. In the morning the pane and shutter of the window were found still open. It was thought that the spirit must have appeared to the dog under a visible form different from any thing he had ever before seen; which had been the cause of those unusual agitations; and that this must have been the last visit that the deceased had promised to make his daughter. The next day she actually received a letter from her husband, in which he wrote every thing that had passed at Crecy till the time of her father's decease. By this letter it appeared that he died at Crecy the same day and at the same hour as the apparition was heard at Paris. She ordered several masses to be said for the repose of his soul, since which time nothing has been either seen or heard supernatural in the house.

This fact is taken from a manuscript of Mr. Barry, auditor of accounts.

*A Spectre loaded with Chains appearing to a Young Gentleman,
who courageously followed it into a Garden, where it pointed out to
him the spot where the bones of a person in Chains were actually
discovered.*—A FACT.

ABOUT the year 1570, a young man named Vasques d'Ayola, having gone to Boulogne with two of his companions to study the law, and not having found a lodging in the city to his wishes, they took an apartment in a spacious and magnificent house, but deserted on account of a spectre which frightened every body that came to reside there. They laughed at this discourse, and took up their abode.

At the end of the first month d'Ayola watching alone in his chamber while his companions were sleeping quietly in their beds, he heard a noise at a distance similar to chains dragging along the ground. It appeared advancing towards him up the stairs. He recommended himself to God, made the sign of the cross, took a sword and buckler, and having a taper in the other hand, he saw the door opened by a horrible spectre, nothing but bones, but loaded with chains. Ayola conjured him and asked him what he wanted. The fantom made signs for him to follow him; he accordingly did; but on going down stairs his candle going out, he went back to light it and followed the spirit, which conducted him along a yard where there was a well. Ayola was fearful lest he should precipitate him into it, and stopped: the spectre made signs for him to follow him: they went into the garden, when the fantom disappeared. Ayola plucked up a few handfuls of grass about the spot and returned to relate to his companions what had happened to him. In the morning information was given of it to the principal citizens of Boulogne.

They went to reconnoitre the place and made the most

diligent search. The bones of a corse was found there and loaded with chains. Every enquiry was made but they were never able to discover any thing certain as to the fact. Suitable obsequies was made for the deceased, the remains were interred, and from that time the house was no longer haunted.

This fact is related by Antoine Formequade, in his work intituled: *Les Fleurs curies*.

A troop of Spirits seen wandering at Narni in the middle of the day.

SOME years before the death of Pope Leo the ninth, who died in the year 1059, an infinite multitude of people cloathed in white were seen passing through the city of Narni, and advancing towards the east. This troop kept marching from the morning early until three in the afternoon; but towards evening they perceptibly declined. At this spectacle the whole city mounted the walls, fearing lest they might be a troop of enemies, and saw them file off with an extreme surprize.

A citizen more resolute than the others went out of the city, and having remarked in the crowd a man of his acquaintance, he called him by his name, and asked him, what that multitude of travellers meant; he replied,—"We are souls, who not having expiated all our sins, and not being yet pure enough to enter into the kingdom of heaven, we are going thus into the holy places with a spirit of repentance; we are just come from visiting the tomb of St. Martin, and are going now to Notre Dame at Farfe." The man was so terrified at this vision that he kept his bed for a whole twelvemonth. It was he himself who related the circumstance to Pope Leo the ninth. The whole city of Narni was witness of this procession, which took place in the face of day.

The Ghost of Brutus appearing to him before his death.

ONE night very late, every body sleeping in the camp of Brutus, as he was in his pavilion with very little light, reflecting on something very profoundly within himself, he thought he heard somebody coming in, and casting his eyes towards the entrance of his pavilion he perceived a monstrous and hideous figure of a human body emaciated, withered, horrible, which presented itself to him without saying a word. However Brutus, without being astonished any farther at this vision, asked him with a firm tone of voice, "whether he was human or divine, and what brought him there." The fantom replied,—"I am thy destroying angel, Brutus, you shall see me again at Philippi."—Brutus without any more concern, replied coolly,—"Well, I will meet you there then."—When the fantom disappeared. On the night which preceded the death of Brutus, a little before he gave battle to Antony and Octavian at Philippi, where he slew himself with his own hands the same fantom presented itself to him a second time in the same shape and figure, and then disappeared without uttering a word.

This fact is related by Plutarch and Appian in the fourth book of the Civil Wars, Chapter the last.

*A Young Lady murdered by an evil Spirit through her impious
wishes, and afterwards transformed into a Black Cat.*

ON the 27th day of May 1582, in the capital city of the
duchy of Brabant called Antwerp, and in the Flemish
language Opdemer, lived an extremely beautiful young lady
of a very opulent family, which rendered her the means of
giving full scope to her sensual desires; proud and haughty,
her every moment was engaged at the toilet. Being one day
invited to the nuptials of one of her father's friends, she
piqued herself in outvieing the rest of the ladies in
magnificence and beauty; to effect which she decorated and
attired herself in a most brilliant dress, not forgetting above
all things to add new lustre to her charms by the assistance of
rouge and other different cosmetics, so liberally used by the
Italian courtezans; and in order to elucidate that,
sumptuousness and superstition of bravado (as the Flemish
ladies so much esteem fine linen) she ordered four or five
ruffs to be made, of cambric that cost her nine crowns and a
half the ell. The ruffs being finished she sent for a clear-
starcher in the city, to whom she begged for her to get her
up two of them in the most magnificent stile, in order to
serve her for the clay of the nuptials, and the succeeding one,
promising her as a gratuity the liberal recompence of twenty-
four sous. The good woman executed her commands with
the greatest care and punctuality; still they were not done to
her satisfaction; she sent immediately for another person of
the same profession, to whom she delivered the said articles,
promising her if they were got up to her wishes three times
the sum she had paid before: this second clear-starcher
exerted her utmost to satisfy the ambition of her employer;
but she was unfortunately less successful than the former; as
when she brought them home, the young lady not finding

26

them to her wishes, flew into the most violent rage, threw them on the floor, swearing and blaspheming the name of the Almighty, that she had sooner go to the devil, than to the wedding in things so barbarously executed. The enraged young creature had no sooner finished those words but the devil, who was lying in wait, having assumed the appearance of one of her favourite admirers presented himself before her, having a ruff round his neck very handsomely adjusted; the unfortunate seeing him, and taking him to be one of her principal favourites, addressed herself to him in the most engaging language, and said, "Who has plaited your ruff in such a bewitching stile; that is just the manner in which I wished mine?" The evil spirit momentarily replied, that he had plaited it himself; so saying, he took it off his neck and put it joyfully upon hers; then to complete the stratagem feigned to salute her, and seizing the poor unfortunate round the waist, with a horrible shriek twisted furiously her neck, and left her breathless and inanimate upon the floor. The scream was so loud that being heard by the father and every body in the house, they immediately concluded that some misfortune had happened. On going up into the room they found her extended lifeless upon the ground, having her neck and face bruised and discoloured, insomuch, that all those who looked upon that strange adventure were so affrighted that their hair stood on end with horror upon their heads. The father and mother bewailed their loss most bitterly, and with abundant sighs lamented the disaster of their daughter. After having consulted what was the best to be done, they ordered her to be put in a coffin and interred, lest they should incur dishonour on their family. They gave their neighbours to understand that an apoplexy had carried off their daughter suddenly. But the Almighty, who sends no affliction without a cause, would not suffer such a thing to be concealed and buried in the tomb of oblivion; ordered it to be manifested to every one, that it might serve as an example to posterity. For as the interment was about to take place with every pomp, four strong and powerful men could neither lift nor move the coffin from the bier. The father seeing that, gave orders for two more to come to their assistance; but it was in vain, for the coffin was so ponderous that it seemed as though it were riveted for ever: seeing which, the company freezed with horror, with one common accord concluded that it should be opened, it was instantly done; but at the opening, it was found, to contain nothing but a black cat which leaped out immediately; and disappeared without any one's knowing what became of her.

The disconsolate father frustrated in his attempt, was obliged to declare how every thing had happened, to the disgrace of their family, and to the confusion and condemnation of their dissolute daughter.

The ghost of an old gentleman in chains, appearing to the philosopher Athenodore, (a fact related by Pliny.)

THERE was at Athens a very magnificent house but uninhabited, on account of a spectre which was said to haunt it. The philosopher Athenodore, arriving in that city, and having seen a written paper that signified the house was to be sold and at a low price, purchased it, and went to sleep there with his domestics. As he was occupied in reading and writing during the greatest part of the night, he heard suddenly a great noise, as if chains were dragging along, and perceived at the same time the spirit of an old man loaded with chains, which advanced towards him. Athenodore continued writing, the spectre made signs for him to follow it: the philosopher in his turn made signs for it to stop, and pursued his studies; at length he took his lamp and followed the ghost, which conducted him in the yard, then sunk into a chasm of the earth, and disappeared.

Athenodore, without the least fear, took up a stone to mark the place and returned to his chamber to repose. On the following day he informed the magistrates of what had happened; they went into the house and searched diligently in the place he had pointed out; the bones of a dead body loaded with chains were discovered which were afterwards interred, and the house was undisturbed in future.

This fact is related by Pliny the Younger (Plin. junior. Epist. ad Suram, lib. 7, c. 27.

The spirit of the Marquis de Rambouillet appearing to his friend the Marquis de Precy, as by appointment when alive.

THE marquis of Rambouillet, eldest brother of the duchess of Montanzier, and the marquis of Precy, the eldest of the house of Nantouillet, both from twenty-five to thirty years of age, were intimate friends, and went to battle as was the custom of every person of quality in France. As they were one day in conversation about the affairs of the other world, after much discourse, which was sufficiently expressive that they were not too well persuaded of every thing that is said concerning it, they promised each other that the first who died would come and bring every intelligence to his companion. At the expiration of three months the marquis of Rambouillet set out for Flanders, where the seat of war was at that time; while de Precy, attacked with a violent fever, was detained at Paris. Six weeks after, de Precy heard the curtains of his bed draw aside, and turning himself to see what it was, he perceived the marquis de Rambouillet in boots and regimentals. He jumped out of bed and was going to leap round his neck, to express the joy he felt at his return; but Rambouillet drawing a few paces back, told him that his caresses were no longer necessary, that he had only come to acquit himself of his word which he had given him; that he had been slain the evening before in battle; that every thing that was said of the other world was exceeding true; that he must think of living in another manner, and that he had no time to lose as he would be killed shortly himself. No one can express the surprise that the marquis de Precy experienced at this discourse; not being able to believe what he heard, he made another effort to embrace his friend, whom he thought was deceiving him; Rambouillet seeing that he was incredulous, pointed to the place where he had received his wound, which was in the groin, from whence the blood appeared to flow. After that the fantom vanished and left de Precy in a fright more easy to comprehend than describe. He called at the same time his valet and alarmed the whole house by his shrieks.

Several persons ran to his assistance, to whom he related what he had just seen; every one around him attributed this vision to the ardor of the fever, which might have turned his brain. They intreated him to go to bed again, remonstrating with him that he must have dreamed of what he had said. The marquis much wounded to think he should be taken for a fanatic, related every circumstance a second time; but it was in vain for him to protest that he had seen and heard his friend, they still continued in the same opinion, till the arrival of the post from Flanders, by which they learnt the death of the marquis de Rambouillet. That former circumstance being found consistent with truth and the manner in which de Precy had related it, those to whom he had told the adventure began to believe that there might be something in it, as Rambouillet was killed precisely at the hour, and on the preceding evening that he had mentioned it: it was impossible that he had learnt it through a natural cause. This event being spread abroad in Paris, they thought it was the effect of a troubled imagination, or a tale fabricated for amusement; but whatever persons might say who examined the thing seriously, there was always a suspicion in their minds which nothing but time could by any means eradicate. That depended upon what happened to the marquis de Precy who was menaced to perish in a short time after: consequently every body looked upon his destiny as the denouemant of the piece; however he very soon confirmed their doubts; for as soon as he recovered from his indisposition, the civil wars broke out; he insisted on going to the battle of St. Antoine, although his father and mother who feared the prophecy, did every thing they could to dissuade him from it; he was slain there to the great regret of all his family.

The death of Carlostadt, announced by a spectre that seized his youngest child and threatened to dash his brains out: afterwards ordered him to tell his father to prepare himself, as he should call again in three days.

THE death of Carlostadt was accompanied by the most horrid circumstances according to the testimony of the ministers of Bale his colleagues. They relate (Mostrovius, page 22) that at the last sermon which Carlostadt delivered in the temple of Bale, a tall black figure came and seated himself beside the consul. The preacher perceived it and appeared much troubled. On descending from the pulpit he enquired who the stranger was that had taken his place by the chief magistrate: nobody had seen him. Carlostadt heard of the spectre on his return home a second time.

It had been there, and had seized the youngest and the most tenderly beloved of his children by the hair of his head. After having lifted him from the ground, it made as though it were going to dash his brains out; however it contented itself by ordering the child to inform his father, that in three days it should return, and that he must hold himself in readiness. The child having related to his father what it had said, Carlostadt went to bed in the most dreadful horrors, and expired on the third day after.

The awful dream of Xerxes, the king of Persia.

XERXES, king of Persia, deliberating in a council, whether he should wage war against Greece, was very much dissuaded from it by Artabanes his paternal uncle. Xerxes highly offended at the liberty he had taken, gently reproached him for it. The night following he reflected seriously upon the reasons of Artabanes, and changed his resolution; having fallen asleep, he dreamt he saw a man of an extraordinary stature and deportment who said to him—"You have then renounced the design of making war against the Greeks, although you have issued your orders to the Persian chiefs in order to assemble your army?—you have not done right to change your resolution, although you found no one of your opinion; go, believe me, follow your designs:"—having said that the vision disappeared. The next morning he convened his council a second time, and without speaking of the dream that he had had, he confessed that he was very sorry for what he had said in his anger the day preceding to Artabanes his uncle; declared that he had renounced making war against the Grecians: those of his council overjoyed, prostrated themselves in his presence, and felicitated him for it.

The night following he had for the second time the same vision, and the same phantom said to him—"Son of Darius, thou hast then abandoned the design of declaring war against the Greeks, without taking any notice of what I said to thee? know that if you do not undertake instantly that expedition, you will shortly be reduced to a condition as servile as that which you now enjoy is elevated." The king threw himself off the bed immediately, and sent in haste to fetch Artabanes, to whom he related the two dreams that he had two nights successively; he added "I intreat you to invest yourself with my regal ornaments; to seat yourself upon my throne, then to sleep in my bed; and should the phantom which appeared to me appear to you likewise, I shall think the thing is ordained by the gods decrees, and I will obey their orders."

It was in vain for Artabanes to refuse investing himself with the insignias of royalty; to seat himself upon the king's throne, and to sleep in his bed; alledging that all that would be useless, if the gods had resolved to make him acquainted with their wishes; that, that even would be more capable to irritate the gods, as they wished to make their illusion by those exterior marks; that as to the rest, dreams of themselves deserved not the least attention; and that in common, they were only consequences of representations impressed strongly on the mind the evening before.

Xerxes was not persuaded by these reasonings, and Artabanes did as the king desired, being well assured that if the thing presented itself more than once, it would be a proof of the wish of the gods of the reality of the vision, and of the truth of the dream; he then slept in the king's bed, and the same phantom appeared to him and said; "It is then you who prevent Xerxes executing his resolution, and accomplishing what is decreed by the fates? I have declared to the king what he has to fear if he defers obeying my orders." At the same time it appeared to Artabanes as though it wanted to put out his eyes with a burning iron; he immediately got out of bed and related to Xerxes what had appeared to him, and added; "I change absolutely my opinion; since it pleases the gods that we should make war, and that the Greeks are threatened with great misfortunes, give your orders, and make all your arrangements for war." Which was immediately executed.

The ghost of Desfontaines, appearing to his friend Mr. Bezuel to inform him that he had been drowned, according to a reciprocal agreement.

A VENERABLE priest of the city of Vallonia named Bezuel, being invited to dinner on the 7th of January, 1708, at the house of a lady, a relation of the abbot de St. Pierre; with this abbot, he related to them, according to their desire, a circumstance concerning the apparition of one of his companions whom he had seen in open day, about twelve years from that period.

In 1695, said Mr. Bezuel, being a school-boy about fifteen years of age, I formed an acquaintance with the two children of d'Abaguene, a lawyer, who were school-boys like myself. The eldest was about my age, the youngest was eighteen months less; his name was Desfontaines; we took our walks and all our parties of pleasure together; and whether Desfontaines possessed more friendship for me, or whether he was more gay, more complaisant, more lively than his brother, I was most partial to him.

In 1696, walking in the cloister of the Capuchins, he told me that he had lately read a story concerning two friends who had promised each other that he who should die the first should come and tell his situation to the living; that the deceased appeared to him, and told him the most surprizing things. Upon that Desfontaines said that he had a favour to request of me; which was to make him a similar promise, and that on his side he would make me one; I told him that I would not. He was several months speaking to me of it, often, and very seriously; I still resisted. At length about the month of August, 1696, as he was about departing to the university at Caen, he pressed me so much with tears in his eyes that I consented: he took from his pocket at the same time two little papers that he had written for the purpose, the one signed with his blood, in which he promised me in case of death, to come and give me an account of his situation after death, the other in which I promised him the same thing. I pricked my finger, a drop of blood came with which I signed my name; he was overjoyed to have my letter, and embracing me for it, he returned me a thousand thanks.

Some time after, he departed with his brother. Our separation occasioned us much grief; we wrote to each other every opportunity, and about six weeks after I received his last letter, there happened to me what I am going to relate.

The 31st of July, 1697, one Thursday, I shall remember it to my latest hour; the late Mr. Sortoville with whom I lodged, and who behaved with great kindness to me, begged of me to go into a meadow near the Cordeliers, and to assist him in looking over his people who were making hay. I had not been there a quarter of an hour when about half past two, I felt myself almost stunned by an invisible blow, and was taken with a fainting; in vain did I lean upon my hay fork, they were obliged to lay me upon the ground where I was extended upwards of an hour before I recovered my senses. That passed over, but as nothing before that had ever happened to me I was very much alarmed, and feared lest I was going to be indisposed; however it left but a trifling impression on me the remainder of the day; it is true that at night I slept less than ordinary.

The next day about the same hour as I was leading to the meadow the grandson of Mr. de Sortoville, who was at that time ten years of age, I found myself on the road attacked with a similar fainting; I seated myself upon a stone under the shade. That passed over, and we continued our route: nothing more happened to me that day, and in the night I slept but very little.

In fine, on the morrow, the 2d day of August, being in the barn precisely at the same hour, I was taken with a like dizziness and langour, but more serious than the others; I fainted and lost my senses; one of the servants perceived it: I have been told they asked me at that time what was the matter with me, and that I answered, I saw what I never could have believed; but I neither recollect any question or answer; that however accords with what I remember having seen at that time, the figure of a person naked to his waist, but had not the least recollection who he was. They assisted me to descend a ladder; I held fast to the steps; but as I saw Desfontaines my companion at the foot, my head fell between two of the steps, and I lost my senses a second time. They carried me down, and placed me upon a bench close by them. I saw no more of Mr. Sortoville, nor his domestics, although present; but perceiving Desfontaines at the foot of the ladder, who was beckoning me to come to him, I drew aside on my seat as if to make room for him, while those who saw me and whom I did not see, although I had my eyes open, remarked this movement.

As he did not come, I arose to go to him. He advanced towards me, took me by the left arm with his right, and conducted me about thirty paces from thence into a private street, keeping still fast hold of me. The domestics thinking that my dizziness was over, and that I was going to take a walk, went each of them to their business, except a servant-boy who went and told Mr. Sortoville that I was conversing with myself. Mr. Sortoville thought I was inebriated; he advanced, and heard me make several questions and answers, which he has told me since.

I was there about three quarters of an hour discoursing with Desfontaines: "I promised you," said he, "that if I died first, I would come and tell you. I was drowned the day before yesterday in the river at Caen, nearly about this time; I was walking with such and such a person, it was very warm, we took it in our heads to bathe, a sudden languor came over me and I sunk to the bottom. The abbot of Menil-Jean, my companion, plunged in to save me, I seized his foot; but whether he was afraid it might be a salmon, as I held it very fast, or whether he wished to reach speedily the surface of the water, he shook his leg so hard that he gave me a violent blow upon the breast, and threw me to the bottom of the river, which is exceeding deep."

Desfontaines then related to me every thing that had happened while they were walking, and about what they had been conversing. It was in vain for me to ask him any questions relative to his being saved or damned—whether he was in purgatory—whether I was in a state of grace, and whether I should shortly follow him. He continued his discourse as if he had not heard me, or was not willing to hear me.

I drew near several times to embrace him; but it appeared to me as though I embraced nothing. I felt, however, that he grasped me very strongly by the arm; and when I endeavoured to turn my head aside in order not to look at him any longer, as I could not see him without the greatest pain, he shook my arm as if to oblige me to look at him and listen to him.

He appeared to me much taller than I had seen him when living, although he must have grown within the eighteen months that we had not seen each other; it was the same sound of his voice; he seemed to me neither gay nor sorrowful, but in a situation calm and tranquil. He begged of me when his brother returned, to tell him certain things to say to his parents; he entreated me to repeat the seven psalms that he had had in penitence on the preceding Sunday, and which he had not then recited: after that he recommended me a second time to speak to his brother, and then bid me adieu, separating himself from me, saying, "*till then, till then*" which was our usual words when we left each other.

He said at the time he was drowned, his brother, writing a translation, was very loth to let him go alone, fearing some accident might happen to him. He depicted to me so well the spot in which he was drowned, and the tree in the avenue of Louvigni, on the bark of which he had written a few words; that two years after being in company with the late Count de Gotot, one of those who were with him when he was drowned, I indicated to him the very place, and on counting the trees on a certain side that Desfontaines had specified to me, I went straight to the tree and found his writing: he told me likewise that the article concerning the seven psalms was true, and that in coming from confession they were their penitence; his brother told me since that it was true, at that hour he was writing his version, and that he reproached him for not having accompanied his brother.

As I had suffered nearly a month to elapse without being able to do what Desfontaines had told me with respect to his brother, he appeared to me again twice in the forenoon at a country-house, where I was going to dine about a league from hence. I found myself indisposed, I begged that I might be left to myself, that it was nothing, that I would soon return. I went into a corner of the garden. Desfontaines having appeared to me, he reproached me for not having spoken to his brother, and discoursed with me upwards of half an hour without replying to my questions.

On going the next morning to the cathedral of Notre Dame, he appeared to me again, but for less time, and still pressed me to speak to his brother; and left me saying, "*till then, till then*" and making no answer to my questions.

It is a very remarkable circumstance that I had a pain in that part of my arm by which he seized me the first time, until I had spoken to his brother; I was three days and never slept on account of the astonishment I was in. After the first conversation, I told Mr. de Varonville, my neighbour and school-fellow, that Desfontaines had been drowned; that his apparition had just appeared to me to acquaint me of it. He went off immediately to his parents, to know whether it was true. They had just received the intelligence; but through a misunderstanding, he understood it was the eldest son. He assured me that he had read the letter of Desfontaines, and he thought it must be so. I still maintained that it could not be possible, and that Desfontaines himself had appeared to me. He returned, came back, and told me all in tears, that it was but too true.

Nothing has happened to me since, and this strictly my adventure. It has been related differently, but I have never told it in any other manner than the foregoing. The late Count of Gotot has said that Desfontaines appeared also to Mr. Menil-Jean, but of that I am unacquainted. He lives about sixty miles from hence, and that is all I know.

This is a very singular and very circumstantial recital, related by the Abbot de St. Pierre, who is by no means credulous, in the 4th vol. p. 57, of his Political Works.

A Dream told by Cicero concerning two Arcadians who travelling together stopped at Megara, and lodged at different houses. The one of them appeared to the other in a Dream, told him he was murdered by the innkeeper, and begged that he would look in the morning for his body, which was concealed in a waggon.

TWO Arcadians who were travelling together, arrived at Megara, a city of Greece, situated between Athens and Corinth. The one, who had a claim of hospitality in the town, lodged at a friend's house, and the other at an inn. After supper, he who was with his friend, retired in order to go to bed. In his sleep it seemed to him that he who was at the inn appeared to him, and begged him to assist him, as the innkeeper was going to murder him. He rose up immediately much terrified at his dream. However, having collected himself, he fell asleep again, when the other appeared to him a second time, and told him that since he had not had the kindness to assist him, he hoped he would not let his death go unpunished: that the innkeeper after having killed him, had concealed his body in a waggon, and had covered it over with dung; and that he would be sure to find him in the morning at the opening of the city gates, before the waggon went out. Struck with this second dream, he went very early in the morning to the gates, saw the waggon, and asked the man who drove it what he had under the dung. The wagoner immediately took flight, the corpse was taken out of the waggon, and the innkeeper was arrested and punished.

Cicero relates this fact, *(Cicero de divinatione.)*

The Ghost of Humbert Birk, a Flanderkin, that haunted a house in a manner similar to Scratching Fanny.

HUMBERT BIRK, a well known citizen of the town of Oppenheim, and master of a country boarding-school, died in the month of November 1620, a few days before St. Martin. On the Saturday after his obsequies, certain noises were heard in the house where he had lived with his first wife; for when she died, he was re-married to another.

The master of the house suspecting that it was his brother-in-law who was coming, said—"If you are Humbert my brother-in-law, knock three times against the wall." At the same time they heard three blows distinctly, and no more; for in common he paid no respect to number. He was often heard at the fountain when they were going to draw water, and frightened the whole neighbourhood. He did not at all times speak with a very articulate voice, but made himself heard by reiterated blows, by a noise, a palpitation, a groan, a whistle, or by a shriek like a person in distress. The whole of this lasted for the space of six months, when it ceased all of a sudden.

At the expiration of a year, and a little after its anniversary, it was heard more clamorous than before. The master of the house and the most courageous of his domestics, asked it at length what it wanted, and in what they could assist it. It replied with a hoarse and croaking voice, "Order the curate to come with my three children next Saturday." The curate being indisposed, was not able to go on the day appointed; but he went on the Monday following, accompanied by a great number of his friends.

Humbert was informed of it, who replied in the most intelligible manner. They asked him if he wished for mass. He requested it to be said thrice. Whether he wished for any alms to be distributed? He answered, let them give eight bushels of corn to the poor; let my widow give something to all my children. He then ordered them to revise what had been badly distributed in his succession, which was about twenty florins. They asked him why he infested that house in preference to any other? He replied, that he was obliged to it through conspiracies and maledictions: Whether he had received the holy sacrament of the church? I received it from the curate your predecessor. They made him recite to him the *Pater-noster* and the *Ave Maria*. With much difficulty he did, saying that he was prevented from it by a wicked spirit that would not suffer him to say many other things of consequence to the curate.

The priest who belonged to the abbey of All Saints, went to the monastery on Tuesday, Jan. 12, 1621, in order to take the advice of his superiors in so singular an affair; they referred him to three monks to assist him with their counsels. They went together to the house where Humbert was continuing his importunities; as nothing had been executed of what he had requested. A great concourse of the neighbours had assembled there. The master of the house told Humbert to knock against the wall; he accordingly did, but very gently; he told him a second time, "go and fetch a stone, and knock harder;" a silence ensued, as if he had been gone to pick up a stone, a louder blow was heard against the wall; the master whispered to his neighbour as low as possible, for him to knock seven times, which he immediately did. He testified always a great respect for the priests, and never replied to them with the same boldness as he did to the laity; when he was asked the cause of it,—"It is," said he, "that they have the holy sacrament about them; they had never had it before, but on that day they fortunately had, having just said mass. The following day mass was said three times according to his request; they likewise prepared to make a pilgrimage, which he had specified in the last discourse they had with him: they promised also to distribute the alms he so earnestly desired. Since that period Humbert never returned again.

The Spirit of a Gentleman appearing several nights to a Taylor in a cloud of Sulphur.

ON the 9th of September 1625, one John Steinlin died at a place called Altheim, in the diocese of Constantia. Steinlin was a gentleman of an independent fortune, and a counsellor for the city. Some few days after his death his Ghost appeared in the middle of the night to a taylor named Simon Bauh, in the shape of a man surrounded with a gloomy flame, similar to that of lighted sulphur. It continued its visits, but was always silent. Bauh, being much alarmed at his nightly guest, was resolved to ask him what he could do for him. He seized the opportunity on the 17th of November following. As he was reposing one night in his chimney corner, a little after eleven in the evening, he saw the spectre open gently the door, and in its usual flame fix itself before him. The taylor asked it its request: it replied with a ghostly and hollow voice, that he could assist him if he would; but added, "Do not promise me if you are not resolved to execute your promise."—"I will, should they not surpass my power," replied the taylor trembling. "I wish then," resumed the spectre, "for you to order a mass to be said in the chapel of the Virgin of Rottemburgh. I have made a promise for it in my life time, and never acquitted it. You will give orders likewise for two masses to be said at Altheim, the one for departed souls, and the other for the Virgin; and as I have not always been exact in paying my domestics, I wish for a quarter of corn to be distributed to the poor." Simon promised to satisfy its demands. The spirit extended to him his hand, as if to bind the engagement; but Simon fearing lest something might happen to him, presented to it the corner of his seat; the spectre having touched it, made the impression of his five fingers on it, as if it had been scorched by fire. After that it vanished with such a tremendous noise that the report was heard at three houses distance.

This fact is related by a Monk of Toussaint Abbey in the Black Forest.

An invisible Spirit that infested a Printing Office, boxed the ears of the Workmen, threw their hats about the room, pelted them with stones, and committed various acts of mischief.

TOWARDS the end of the year 1746, profound groans were heard proceeding from a corner of a Printing Office of a Mr. Lahart, in the city of Constantia. The workmen only laughed at it at first; but on the year following, about the beginning of January, they heard a louder noise than before, a continual knocking in the same corner where they at first heard only groans. The invisible spectre even went so far as to box the printers' ears, and throw their hats about the office. They had recourse to the capuchin friars, who went with the books proper to exorcise the spirit. The exorcism being completed, they returned home, and the noise ceased for three days.

At the end of that period, the knocking recommenced much louder than before. The spectre threw the letters against the windows. A famous exorcist was sent for from the country, who was fortunate enough to lay the spirit for a whole week. One day the spectre dashed a young man lifeless on the floor, when the letters were seen a second time scattered against the windows. The country exorcist not being able to make any thing of his exorcisms, returned home greatly disappointed.

The spirit continued his tricks, giving boxes of the ears to some, throwing stones, &c. at the others, in such a manner that the compositors were obliged to forsake that corner of the office. They arranged themselves in the middle of the room, but still were the same disturbed.

Other exorcists were sent for, one of whom had a genuine particle of the cross, which he put upon the table. The spirit did not think proper to desist from his usual gaieties, but began boxing the ears of the exorcist and the friar that accompanied him so violently that they were both very happy to leave the company. Others then came, who having mixed a quantity of sand and ashes in a pail of holy water, they scattered it about the floor; and being furnished with swords, they began brandishing them about the room in order to see whether they could strike the spirit, and then looked minutely upon the ground to see whether it had left any vestige of its feet upon the ashes. They at length perceived that it had mounted up the chimney, and observed in several places the vestiges of its feet and hands, imprinted upon the ashes and holy sand.

After various efforts they dislodged it from its hiding place, and in a few moments after found it must have glided under a table, as he had left upon the floor the marks of his feet and hands. The clouds of dust that arose in consequence of this research, occasioned every one to leave the room and give over the pursuit.

However the principal exorcist not being willing to depart dissatisfied, tore up a board in the corner where the groans had first been heard, and found in a little hole, several feathers, three bones wrapt up in a dirty cloth, some pieces of glass, and a bodkin. He repeated several benedictions over a fire which they kindled, and threw the contents into it. But the monk had scarce returned to his convent, when a printer's boy went to inform him that the bodkin had darted out of the fire three times of its own accord, and that a boy who was going to put it into the fire again with a pair of tongs, was struck violently upon the cheek. The remains of what was found had been carried to the convent of the capuchin friars, where they burnt without the least harm arising. Some few days after the infestations re-commenced in the house of the printer; the spectre boxing the ears, throwing stones and molesting the servants in various manners.

Mr. Lahart the master of the house, received a considerable wound in the head: two boys who were sleeping in the same bed, were tumbled upon the ground; so that the whole house was entirely deserted during the night. One Sunday a servant carrying some linen from the house was attacked violently with stones. Another time two boys were precipitated down a ladder. No one was able to account for this extraordinary phenomenon, nor could any of the brotherhood completely lay the spirit; the house in a short time after became uninhabited, and signalized among the number of the haunted.

A Slave supposed to have been cut in pieces through his presumption in conjuring up Devils in an Old Castle at the Isle of Malta.

In the isle of Malta, two knights having purchased a slave, who boasted of his knowing the secret of conjuring up devils, and obliging them to discover the most hidden mysteries, they took him into an old castle where they thought great treasures were concealed. The slave began his conjurations, and in a short time the demon opened a rock, and a massy chest fell out. The slave was going to seize hold of it, but the chest returned back into its place; the thing recommenced more than once; when the slave, after various efforts but in vain, went to the knights and told them what had happened; that he was so much enfeebled by the attempts he had made, that he stood in need of a little brandy, in order to fortify his courage. They gave him some, and in a short time, after having returned., they heard a noise; they went into the cavern with a light to see what had happened, where they found their slave extended lifeless on the earth; his body seemed as though it had been mangled with a pen-knife. The gashes represented a cross. The knights carried him to the borders of the sea, and precipitated him into it with a stone tied round his neck.

This fact is related by sir Guiot de Marre, an inhabitant of the island.

A most extraordinary account of a Ghost that appeared to a Young Man. After lifting up his bed, and removing his bedstead several times, and making the most uncommon noises, threw him into a kind of trance.

MR. S. a young man from twenty-four to twenty-five years of age, resided at St. Maur in the year 1706. After having heard a violent knocking at his door, being in bed without his servant, who ran immediately without seeing any body, and the curtains of his bed drawing, although there was no one but himself in the room. On the 22d of March in the same year, about eleven in the evening having been regulating some papers with three young lads his apprentices; they all heard distinctly a noise like the rolling of papers upon the table; the cat was at first suspected; but Mr. S. having taken a candle and searched diligently found nothing.

Being in bed a short time after, and his boys sleeping in the kitchen, which was attached to his chamber, he heard the same noise as before in his cabinet; he got up to see what it was, and having found nothing more than he did at first, he was going to shut the door, but he felt some resistance, upon which he went in, in order to see whence the obstacle could proceed. He heard at the same moment a noise in one corner, similar to a blow that had been struck against the wall. He screamed out; his servants came to his assistance; he endeavoured to cheer them up, although terrified himself; and having found nothing, he went to bed again and fell asleep. Scarce had the boys put out their light, when Mr. S. was awoke a second time by a sudden shock, similar to that of a boat striking against the arch of a bridge. He was so alarmed that he called his servants, when on their bringing a light he was wonderfully surprised to find his bed removed at least four feet from its original place. He immediately conceived that the shock he had felt proceeded from his bed striking against the wall. His domestics having replaced his bed, saw with as much astonishment as fear, the curtains open all at once, and the bed run towards the chimney. Mr. S. immediately arose, and passed the remainder of the night by his fire-side. About six o'clock in the morning, having made another attempt to sleep, he had no sooner laid down, than the bed made the same movement twice in presence of his attendants, who held the bed-posts to prevent its being displaced. In fine, being obliged to resist any farther, he went to take a walk till dinner; after which having endeavoured to repose himself, and his bed having been twice removed from its situation, he sent for a gentleman who lodged in the same house, as well to cheer his dejected spirits as for him to witness an instance so surprizing; but the shock that took place before the gentleman, was so violent that one of the posts were broken; this alarmed Mr. S. so much that when the gentleman begged that he might see it a second time, he replied, that what he had experienced, together with the dreadful noise that he had heard in the night, were sufficient to convince him of the fact.

Thus the affair, which had till then rested between Mr. S. and his domestics, became public. The report being quickly spread abroad, and having reached the ears of an illustrious prince who had just arrived at St. Maur, his highness was curious to have the mystery unriddled, in consequence of which, he gave himself the trouble to examine minutely into the facts that were related. As this adventure was the subject of every conversation, nothing was heard shortly after but stories concerning ghosts by the most credulous, and pleasantries on the part of others. In the interim Mr. S. was endeavouring to cheer himself up against the night following, and to render himself worthy of conversing with the spectre, as he had no doubt but it had something to say to him. He slept till the next morning, nine o'clock, without having felt any thing more than little liftings up, as if the bed was rising up and down, which only served to rock him and make him sleep the sounder. The next day passed over quietly, but on the 26th the spectre which appeared to have left off his tricks, resumed his sportive disposition, and began in the morning to make a great noise in the kitchen. This, had it rested there, might have been looked over, but about twelve o'clock it grew more violent. Mr. S. who since confest that he had a particular partiality for his cabinet, notwithstanding he had some fears of being there by himself; going into it about six o'clock, he made a few turns to the farther end, and returning towards the door to go to his chamber, was very much surprized to find himself shut up all alone and barricaded with the two bolts. At the same moment the lid of a great chest opened behind him and rendered his cabinet rather dark on account of the window being behind the lid.

This spectacle threw Mr. S. into a terror more easy to imagine than describe; however he had *sang froid* sufficient to hear with his left ear a distinct voice which proceeded from the corner of the cabinet, and which seemed to him about a foot above his head, which spoke to him in very engaging terms for some minutes, and ordered him to do a certain thing, concerning which it recommended secrecy, which he published. It gave him a fortnight to accomplish it; that it commanded him to go in a place where he would find people to instruct him what to do, and that it threatened to return to torment him if he failed in his obedience. Its conversation finished by an adieu.

After this Mr. S. remembers to have fallen into a swoon upon the chest, during which time he felt a pain in his side.

The violent noise and shrieks that he fetched afterwards, occasioned several persons to run to his assistance, who having made useless efforts to open the doors of the cabinet, were proceeding to break it open with a crow, when they heard Mr. S. dragging himself along towards the door, which with much difficulty he opened. In confusion when he appeared, and beyond the power of utterance, they conveyed him to the fire, and then to his bed, where he experienced all the compassion of the illustrious prince of whom we have already spoken, who ran at the first report of this event. His highness having visited every corner of the house without finding any one concealed, wished Mr. S. to be let blood; but his surgeon perceiving his pulse to be very low, thought that it could not be done without danger.

When he recovered from his swoon, his highness, who wished to discover the truth, interrogated him concerning his adventure. Mr. S. protested that he could not without running the risk of his life tell him any more. The spectre did not visit him again for a fortnight, but at the expiration of that term, whether his orders had not been faithfully executed, or whether he was glad to come and thank Mr. S. for his exactitude, as he was one night sleeping in a little bed near to his chamber window, his mother in the great bed, and one of his friends in an arm chair near the fire, they all three heard a violent knocking against the wall, and so great a blow given against the casement, that they thought all the glass was broken. Mr. S. got up immediately and went into his cabinet, in order to see whether the importunate spectre had any thing more to say, but he neither found nor heard any thing. This finished that adventure, which made so much noise and attracted so many of the curious at St Maur.

A tall Spectre that appeared in the air, warning the people of Besanson to amend—when a terrible earthquake ensued, which ingulphed the whole city.

IN the town of Besanson, on the 3d of December 1564, about nine o'clock in the morning, being as fine weather, mild and temperate, and as beautiful a sun as ever shone; a figure of a man was seen in the air about nine feet high, who exclaimed with an awful voice three times, "People, people, people, amend or the end of your days is nigh;" this happened on a market day, in the presence of more than ten thousand persons; after saying these words the figure transformed itself into a naked one, and seemed to retire direct towards heaven. An hour after or thereabouts, a cloud over-shadowed and darkened the atmosphere so much, that for twenty leagues round the city it appeared as though it were completely night; added to that, several persons were taken suddenly ill and died; the miserable inhabitants fell to prayers, forming processions, supplicating the Almighty to appease the weather. The honest villagers came from miles around, bringing their children to the town. At the expiration of three days the most lovely weather succeeded as before; a little while after that the most boisterous wind arose that was ever remembered, which continued for an hour and a half, and such a heavy fall of rain, that it seemed as though it came down in pipes, accompanied with a marvellous earthquake, so that the whole city was ingulphed. And out of the flat country, comprehending the said town, forty miles long and thirty broad, nothing remained but a church, castle, and three houses, which stood in the middle of the city; they are still to be seen in form of a crescent, completely turned towards the east; several relics of the city walls are yet to be seen in the church and castle. Numbers have certified the truth of the above accounts, who even went to the emperor to announce formally these horrible events. In fine, the name of the persons, all inhabitants of the villages of Penay and Guetz, who went to inform the emperor, were named as follows: Mr. de la Pile, Mr. de Courier, John Belon, John Rufin, John Maluen, Stephen Pelisson, Peter Desgras, John Budaulb, John Pouligne, and Thomas Besnier.

The aforesaid village of Penay, was about six miles distant from the city, the inhabitants of which, were so terrified at the earthquake that eleven of them died with fear.

The Spirit of a departed Soul appears to a Countryman, who found
a Vase which contained its Ashes.

THEODORE DE GAZE, had in Campania a little farm, which was cultivated by the assistance of one husbandman alone; as he was tilling the ground he discovered a round vase, in which were enclosed the ashes of a departed soul; a spectre immediately appeared, which commanded him to commit again to the earth the same vase with its contents, or his eldest son should die. The countryman paid no regard to its menaces, when a few days after his son was actually found lifeless in his bed. A short time after the same spectre appeared to him, reiterating to him the same command, and threatened him with the death of his second son. The husbandman told this to his master Theodore, who went himself to the spot and put it carefully in its place.

This fact is related by Le Loyer.

IN 1581 at Dalhem, a village situate between Mozelle and Sarre, one Pierron, a herdsman, married, having one boy, formed a violent attachment for a young girl his neighbour. One day as he was absorbed in thought about her, she appeared to him in the fields, or the demon in her shape. Pierron discovered his passion to her, she promised to accede to his desires on condition that he would give himself up to her and be obedient to her in every thing. Pierron consented to it and consummated his abominable passion with the spectre. Some time after Abrahel, (which was the name the demon assumed), begged as a pledge of his affection, that he would sacrifice to her his only son, and at the same moment gave him an apple for his son to eat, who having tasted of it fell lifeless on the floor. The parents frantic with despair, were inconsolable.

Abrahel appeared to the herdsman a second time, and promised to restore his son to life provided he would grant him the favour to adore him as his God. The peasant fell upon his knees and adored Abrahel, when the child began immediately to breathe: he opened his eyes, they warmed him, rubbed his body, and in about the space of half an hour he resumed the use of his limbs and faculties. He was the same in person as before, excepting more emaciated, more haggard, more feeble; his eyes languid and sunk in; his movements were more slow and embarrassed; his senses more dull and stupid. At the expiration of a twelvemonth, the demon that animated him left him with a violent noise, the youth fell backwards; when his corse infected, and with an insupportable odour, was drawn with a crook out of his father's house and interred without ceremony in a field.

This event was related at Nancy, and examined by the magistrates, who enquired minutely into the fact, heard witnesses, and found the circumstance precisely as above. This account was furnished us by Mr. Nicholas Remy, procurer general of Lorraine.

Two Gentlemen having promised that he who should die first,
should come and inform the other how he approved of immortality;
at his Decease his Spirit actually appeared mounted upon a White
Horse.

MICHAEL MERCATI, prothonotary of St. Siege, a gentleman of known property and very learned, more especially in Platonic philosophy, to which he incessantly applied himself with Marsilus Fiein his friend, as zealous as himself to Plato's doctrine. One day these two great philosophers discoursing upon the immortality of the soul, and whether it staid and existed after the decease of the body. Having discoursed largely upon that subject they promised each other and shook hands, that the first who should depart this world should come and inform the other of his future state.

Having thus separated, it happened some time after, that the same Michael Mercati was wide awake and studying at an early hour in the morning the same subjects of philosophy, he heard a noise all of a sudden, similar to the noise of a cavalier coming in great haste at his door, and at the same time heard the voice of his friend Marsilus, who exclaimed out to him:—"Michael, Michael! Nothing is more true than what has been said of the other world."—Michael immediately opened the window, and saw Marsilus mounted upon a white horse which flew away with him full speed. Michael cried out to him to stop, but he continued his course till he was out of sight.

Marsilus Fiein lived then at Florence, and died there at the same hour that he had appeared and spoken, to his friend. The latter wrote immediately to Florence to inquire into the truth of the fact, when he was informed that Marsilus had departed at [the] same moment as Michael had heard his voice and the sound of his horse at the door. Since that adventure Michael Mercati although very determined in his conduct before, was transformed into another man, and lived in a manner quite exemplary, and as a perfect model of the christian life.

Cardinal Barronius relates this fact. *(Barronius ad an. Christi* 40. *tom. 5, annal.)*

The Apparition of a Man seats himself by his side the Day before his Death.

A SOLDIER being quartered in the house of a Haidamac peasant, on the frontiers of Hungary, saw a stranger come in and seat himself beside his host while they were at table. The master of the house was wonderfully frightened as well as the rest of the company. The soldier knew not what to think, being ignorant as to the result of what had happened. But the landlord expiring on the succeeding day, the soldier enquired into the matter of surprize. He was informed it was the father of his host. who died about ten years prior to that epoch, who had come thus to seat himself beside him, and had announced and occasioned his death.

The soldier at first informed the regiment of it, and the regiment carried the news to the general officers, who commissioned the Count of Cabreras, a captain of a regiment of Alandetti infantry, to enquire into the fact. Having arrived at the place with other officers, a surgeon and a judge, they took down the depositions of all the people of the house, who attested in an uniform manner, that the spectre was the landlord's father, and that every thing that the soldier had said and related was strictly true, which was likewise attested by all the inhabitants of the village.

An Angel appears to a religious Character in a Monastery.

A YOUNG man of very great family named Clarus, and who after having finished his studies was elevated to the order of priesthood, giving himself to the worship of the Almighty in a monastery, conceived he had an open commerce with the angels; and as it is hardly to be believed, he said that on the night following, the Omnipotent would give him a white coat in order that he might appear among them. In fact about twelve o'clock at night the whole monastery seemed as though it were agitated by an earthquake. The cell of the young man appeared most brilliantly illuminated, and a noise as though a number of people were going, coming, and conversing with each other.

After this had taken place he went out of his cell, and presented himself to the friars in the tunic, with which he was invested; it was composed of a stuff of an astonishing whiteness, brilliant, and of an extraordinary fine texture, insomuch that no one was able to say of what substance it was wrought.

The remainder of the night was passed in singing psalms and offering up thanksgivings: in the morning they wanted very much to conduct him to St. Martin; he made every possible resistance, saying that he had been expressly forbidden to appear in his presence. While they were pressing him to go there, the tunic vanished before the eyes of every one present; which proved clearly to all that it must have been an illusion of the demon, who was transforming himself into an angel of light (*Sulpitius Sever. vit. S. Martin,* c.15)

The Spirit of a Philosopher while sleeping transports itself into a distant Country.

A VERY learned character of Dijon, after having been perplexed the whole day upon an important point of a Greek poet without being able to comprehend its meaning, went to repose amidst all his embarrassed thoughts. While he was asleep, his geni transported him in idea to Stockholm, introduced him into the palace of her Christian Majesty, conducted him into the library, and shewed him a little volume, which was precisely the one he was in search of. He opened it, and read ten or a dozen Greek verses, which cleared up actually the difficulty that had impeded him so long. He awoke, and committed to paper the verses that he had seen at Stockholm. The next day he wrote to Mr. Descartes, who was then in Sweden, and begged him to look in such and such a partition of the library, and see whether the book, of which he sent him a description, was there, and whether the Greek verses that he had transmitted were contained in it.

Mr. Descartes wrote him that he had found the book in question, and that the verses were actually in the very place he had pointed out; that one of his friends had promised him a copy of the work, and would send it him the first opportunity.

AN old woman of Malta was informed by a geni, that there was in her cellar concealed a treasure of inestimable value, belonging to a knight of very great distinction, and ordered her to inform him of it. She went, but found it impossible to obtain an audience. The night following, the same geni returned; gave her a similar charge; and on her refusing to obey he ill treated her, and sent her back a second time. On the following day she went to the nobleman again, and told the servants that she would not leave the house until she had seen their master. She related to him what had happened to her; upon hearing this the knight resolved to go home with her, accompanied by a number of persons furnished with pickaxes and other instruments used in digging up the earth. They dug, and in a very little time such a torrent of water issued from the fracture they had made, that they were obliged to give up their enterprize.

The knight went, and confessed to the inquisitor what he had done, and received absolution. Still he was obliged to write in the registers of the inquisition the fact we have just related.

About sixty years after, the canons of the cathedral at Malta being desirous of forming before their church a more extensive square, purchased several houses in order to pull down, and amongst others that which had belonged to the old woman. Digging there they found the treasure which consisted of several pieces of gold about the value of a ducat, bearing the effigy of Justin I. The Lord Steward of Malta pretended that the treasure belonged to him, as sovereign of the island: the canons contested it with him. The affair was carried to Rome: the Lord Steward gained his cause: the gold was brought to him, to the value of about sixty thousand ducats. However he gave them to the cathedral church.

Some time after the knight of whom we have spoken, who was then very much in years, remembering what had happened, pretended that the treasure ought to belong to him. He ordered himself to be conducted to the spot, recognized the cave in which he had formerly been, and pointed out in the registers of the inquisition what he had written there sixty years before. That, however, did not enable him to recover the treasure; still it was a convincing proof that the demon was acquainted with, and presided over, the money.

A Spirit convinces a Philosopher in a Dream of the immortality of the Soul.

A PHYSICIAN named Genirade, a great friend of St. Augustin, and well known at Carthage by his extensive genius and his benevolence to the poor, doubted there was any other life after this. One night he saw in a dream a young man, who said,—"follow me."—he followed him in idea, and went into a city, where he heard on his right an astonishing melody; he had not the least remembrance of what he saw on his left.

Another time, he saw the same young man, who said to him; "Do you recollect me?" "Exceeding well," replied he. "And how came you to know me?" He then related to him every thing that this youth had shewn him in the city into which he had conducted him. The young man added, "Was it then in a dream or awake that you saw all this?"—"In a dream," said he; "And what I am saying to you now, do you hear it in a dream or awake?" "In a dream," replied he. "How is it then possible for you to see me?" As he was hesitating, and knew not how to answer, the young man resumed; "Just as you see and hear me now your eyes are closed, and your senses are asleep, shall you after death, live, see, and hear, but with the faculties of the spirit; therefore never form a doubt that there is no life after this.—This event is related by St. Augustin.

A Book flies from one place to another, and opens by an invisible hand.

WHEN Mr. Patris accompanied Mr. Gaston in Flanders, he resided in the castle of Egmont: the hour for dinner being arrived, and on going out of his chamber to the room in which they dined, he stopped as he was passing the door of an officer belonging to Mr. Gaston's regiment, in order to take him with him: he knocked tolerably hard; seeing the officer did not come he knocked again, and called him at the same time, asking him whether he did not mean to come to dinner. The officer made no answer; Patris having no doubt but he was in his room, as the key was in the door, opened it, and on going in, saw him sitting at his table like one distracted; he went up to him and asked him what he was about. The officer recovering himself, said "You would not be less surprized than myself, if you had seen as well as I, that book you see yonder fly there of its own accord, and the leaves turn over of themselves, without beholding any thing farther." It was a philosophical work of Cordan, concerning the subtility of matter. "Come, come," said Mr. Patris, "you are only jesting, your imagination filled with what you had just read, you must have got up and put the book in the place where it is, and on sitting down again with your senses absorbed, and not finding the book before you, you have thought it went there of itself." "What I tell you," replied the officer, "is very true, and as a proof that it was no vision, out of that door, which was opened and shut, the ghost retired." Mr. Patris went to open the door he spoke of, which took him into a long gallery, at the end of which, there was a wooden chair so heavy which must have been impossible for two of the strongest men to lift. This chair was seen to move of its own accord, and quitting its place, came straight towards him, as if supported in the air: terrified at this prodigy, Mr. Patris exclaimed out, "Mr. Devil, the concerns of God apart, I am very much your servant; but I beg of you not to frighten me any more;" upon which the chair returned into its place. This made a very strong impression upon the mind of Mr. Patris, and did not a little contribute to inspire him with religion.—Mr. Segrais makes mention in his historical remarks of this event, who says he learnt it from Mr. Patris himself, who was a gentleman worthy of belief, and who related it to him in the most serious manner possible.

The Apparition of a Woman after her decease visits and torments
her Daughter.

BEFORE and after Easter in the year 1700, an apparition made
its appearance in the house of Mr. Vidi, a tax gatherer of
Dourdaus, which commenced by making a noise in a room
at a distance from any other, which was appropriated to the
use of one of his servants, who happened to be indisposed;
the poor girl frequently heard the most profound groans,
similar to those of a person in distress, but saw nor felt
nothing. She laid under these miserable apprehensions of fear
nearly for the space of six months. When she was recovered
Mr. Vidi sent her to her father's, in order to breathe her
native air; she staid there about a month, during which time
she neither saw nor heard any thing extraordinary.

At the expiration of which time, she returned home in
perfect health, except that of having a rash, being the relics of
her disorder. Mr. and Mrs. Vidi ordered her again to sleep in
the little room; the sound of these words so alarmed her, that
she told them she must absolutely be excused, as she had
frequently heard a noise there. Two or three days after being
in an outhouse, where she went to fetch some wood, she felt
something pull her by the petticoat. After dinner on the same
day, Mrs. Vidi sent her to hear a particular mass which is said
after Easter; as she was coming out of the church, she felt the
invisible spectre pull her with such violence by the petticoat,
that she stood for some time motionless. An hour after this
she returned home, and on going into her mistresses room,
she was attacked a third time in the same familiar stile. Mrs.
Vidi perceiving her terrified enquired into the cause, when
the poor unfortunate told her how she had been beset at
different times, and at that very moment she had been caught
hold of by an unknown hand: Mrs. V. looking at her

stedfastly, perceived that several plaits of her petticoat were torn out behind, and that a clasp that fastened it was broken. The girl had at that time both her hands engaged.

Mrs. V. seeing this prodigy shuddered at it with horror, and told the servant to go immediately into an antichamber, and put down that which she had in her hands. As she was going out of the room the spectre pulled her very hard again: this was on a Friday evening. On Sunday night as soon as she was in bed, she heard it walking in her chamber, and a short time after that the spectre came and laid itself by her side, and passed a hand over her face of a deathly coldness as if it wanted to caress her. She took her rosary which was in her pocket, and put it round her neck. Mr. and Mrs. Vidi had told her on the day preceding, that if she continued hearing any thing, for her to conjure the spirit in the name of God to explain itself to her, which she did mentally; the terror she was in at that awful moment having deprived her of her speech. She then heard a muttering noise, but nothing articulate. Between three and four in the morning the spectre made so great a noise that it seemed as though the house was falling down. This awoke every body. Mrs. Vidi called her *fille de chambre* to go and see what it was, thinking it might have been the servant. They found her in a dripping perspiration; she dressed herself all but her stockings, which she could not find. She went in that state into Mr. and Mrs. V.'s chamber, who saw a cloud of smoke similar to a fog that followed her and disappeared in a moment after. She made them a recital of every thing that had taken place. They told her to get herself in readiness, and as soon as the bells rang for mass at five o'clock she must go to confess and receive the sacrament. She went to fetch her stockings that she could not find. Her mistress told her to search every where under the bed, which she did, but she found them thrown upon the tester: she reached them down with a long stick. She found her shoes set upright against the window, and observed that one of the windows was open. When she had resumed her senses she went to confess and receive the sacrament. On her return, Mr. Vidi asked her what she had done. She told him that as soon as she went to the communion table she saw her mother by her side, who looked just the same as she did in her illness although she had been dead eleven years. After the communion she retired into a chapel, where she had no sooner entered, but her mother fell upon her knees before her and took hold of her hands saying,—"Daughter, be not afraid, I am your mother. Your brother was burnt by an accident while I was at the lord of the manor's oven at Oisonville, near d'Etampes. I went immediately to the good old curate of Garanecirs to ask a penitence, thinking that misfortune was occasioned through my neglect. He would not give it me, saying I was not culpable, and sent me to the penitentiarist at Chartres. I went to him, and he refused in the same manner to give me one; but as he saw that I persisted in having one, that which he imposed upon me was, to wear a horse-hair girdle for two years, which I was unable to execute on account of my pregnancies and indispositions. Being now dead will you fulfill this penance for me?" The daughter promised she would. The mother then charged her to fast upon bread and water four Fridays and Saturdays, to order mass to be said at Gromerville, to pay to one Lanier, a miller, twenty-six sous which she owed him for flour, that he had sold her; and to go into the cellar of the house where she died; that she would find the sum of seven livres which she had concealed under the first step; that if the person to whom the house then belonged would not suffer her to look there, she was not to force him, as she was not in pain for it; to make a journey to Chartres for her to the church of *Notre dame,* and that she would yet speak to her once more. She made her many remonstrances, telling her that she must pray to the Virgin Mary, that God would refuse her nothing, that penance in this world was very easy to perform; but that in the other was very difficult.

On the next day she ordered a mass to be said, during which time the spectre took off her beads. The same day it took hold of her hand and pressed it most affectionately. The two following days she saw it standing by the side-board while Mr. and Mrs. Vidi were at supper; her master perceiving her look chilled with horror while the big drops ran trickling down her cheeks, he made signs to her to know what was the matter. She told him that she saw her mother; and on the next day when there was not so many people, she shewed Mr. and Mrs. Vidi that it was still in the same place, but they saw nothing. Mr. Vidi thought it was expedient for her to acquit as soon as possible her mother's obligations; on that account he sent her the first opportunity to Gromerville, where she gave orders for a mass, payed the twenty-six sous which were actually due, and found the seven livres which were under the third step of the cellar as the spectre had indicated. From thence she went to Chartres, where she ordered three masses to be said and received the sacrament in the choir. As she was coming out her mother appeared to her a second time, saying "daughter will you do all I told you?" The daughter replied yes, at the same time she said to her;—"I shall acquit myself and charge you with it in my place. I bid you adieu, speak not to me, I am going to eternal glory."

Since that period the girl neither saw nor heard any thing more. She wore the horse-hair girdle night and day for two years as her mother had recommended.

This fact, taken from a manuscript of Mr. Barce, was written December 15, 1700, by Mr. Vidi to Mr. Quindre his friend at Orleans.

This Historical Tract, respecting Charles le Chauve, related by himself in Latin, was extracted from the manuscripts 2447, belonging to the National Library, in folio, page 188. The translation is as follows.

ONE Sunday night returning from matins, as this prince was going to repose, an awful voice murmured in his ears. "Charles thy spirit is going to leave thy body, thou shalt come and see the judgments of the Omnipotent, which shall serve thee either as a preservative or presage. Thy spirit nevertheless shall be rendered to thee some time after. At that moment his spirit was ravished from him, and the spectre that bore it away was of a splendid whiteness. He put into his hand a clew of thread which cast forth an extraordinary light very similar to that of a comet. He unwound it and said, "Take this thread and tie it fast to the thumb of your right hand; by which means I will conduct you into the infernal labyrinths."

This being done he walked before me with an astonishing swiftness, said the king, but kept unwinding this clew of luminous thread, he conducted me into profound vallies of fire and full of burning pits, where pitch, sulphur, lead, wax, and other unctuous matters were bubbling up. I remarked the prelates who had served my father and ancestors. Although trembling I did not fail interrogating them to learn the cause of their torments. They replied, "we have been bishops of your father and ancestors, and instead of exciting in them peace and union, we have only sown amongst them discord and trouble. On that very account we are engulphed in these subterraneous caverns with homicides and thieves. It is here your bishops will come and all that numerous train of officers that surround you and imitate us in evil.

While the king all in a tremble, was considering these things, he perceived a great number of black and horrible monsters, who with crooks and flaming swords fell upon him in order to seize the clew of thread from the hands of the prince; but the extreme light that it cast prevented them from taking it. These same demons wanted to seize the king behind and precipitate him into the pits of sulphur, but the conductor guarded him carefully from the snares they were then extending for him, and led him upon the top of lofty mountains, from whence the torrents of fire arose which melted and kept in a boiling state all kinds of metals. There, said the king, I found the souls of lords who had served my father and brothers; some were plunged over their heads, others up to the chin, and others to the middle of their waist. They then exclaimed, addressing themselves to me, "Alas! Charles you see how we are punished in these torrents of flames, for having sown trouble and division between your father, brothers and yourself!" I cannot however help, continued king Charles, bewailing their misfortunes. At the same time I saw dragons darting at me with their fiery mouths endeavouring to engulph me, but my conductor fortified me by the clew of thread with which he surrounded me, and the extraordinary light so dazzled the dangerous animals that they could not reach me. We then descended into a valley, the ore of which was dismal and obscure, but notwithstanding filled with burning furnaces: I found the opposite side very light and pleasant.

I endeavoured particularly to examine the obscure side; there I saw kings of my own race tormented with strange punishments. My heart devoured by *ennui* and grief, I thought every moment of being precipitated headlong into the same gulph, by gloomy monsters, that set the whole valley in flames. Fear did not forsake me. However by the means of this luminous clew; I perceived that the other side of the valley began to grow lighter, when I remarked two fountains, the water of one was very warm, and the other more mild and temperate. By means of the luminous clew which conducted me, I observed two casks each of them filled with these different waters. In the one I saw my father Lewis, who was plunged up to his waist. Although overwhelmed with grief and sorrow, he kept cheering up my spirits, and said; my dear son Charles, fear nothing, I know your spirit will return into your body; it is the Almighty who has permitted you to come here in order to see me suffer for my sins, from this cask of boiling water, I am conveyed from day to day, into that of a mild and moderate heat. It is a consolation that I owe to the prayers of St. Peter, St. Dennis and St. Remy, who are the protectors of our royal house; but through your prayers, offerings, alms, you can assist me, you my faithful bishops, abbots, and even all the ecclesiastical order, when I shall not be long before I am delivered from this boiling cask. Your brother Lothario and Lewis his son, have been exempt from these punishments through the intercession of St. Peter, St. Dennis and St. Remy; and they now enjoy all the delights of paradise. Look on your left, says my father to me; I immediately turned my head and I observed two large and spacious casks of boiling water. "Behold to what thou art destined, continued he, if you do not correct yourself and do penance for your crimes." Dread seized me instantaneously, when my guide who perceived it, said, "Follow me into the part which is on the right of this valley, wherein is found all the glory of paradise." I did not walk far, before I saw in the midst of the most illustrious of kings, my uncle Lothario, seated upon a topa of an extraordinary size, and crowned with a rich diadem. His son Lewis was in splendor just as brilliant; scarce had he perceived me when with an affectionate voice he called to me and spoke in the following terms; "Charles, who are my third successor in the Roman Empire, approach." I know, continued he, that you are come in these places of torment and trouble, where your father and brother have yet to suffer a considerable time. But by the mercy of God they will be delivered from their sufferings at last, in the same manner as we were extricated from ours, through the prayers of St. Peter, St. Dennis and St. Remy; whom God has established as the patrons of monarchs and the French nation. And had they not been our protectors our family would have been no longer on the throne. Know then that it will not be long before you are dethroned, after which you shall live a little while. Lewis turning himself towards me, the Roman Empire, said he, which you have possessed till now, must pass incessantly into the hands of Lewis my daughter's son: at that very moment I perceived the youth. Commit to him then the sovereign authority, continued Lewis, and give him proofs of it, by entrusting him with the clew that you now hold. I immediately detached it from my hand to give him. By that he was invested with the empire, and the whole clew was in his hand. Scarce was he master of it, but he became arrayed in robes of light; and what is very singular, my spirit returned into my body. Thus the whole world will see in despight of earthly struggles, that he will possess the whole Roman Empire that God has destined to him, and I shall have passed to another life: this shall the Lord execute, whose power extends to all ages over the living and the dead. Amen.

The Ghost of a Nobleman appears in armour to his Commander
under whose service he had lost his life.

A GENTLEMAN named Humbert, the son of a nobleman named Guichard, of Belioc, in the diocese of Macon, having one day declared war with some other noblemen of his neighbourhood, a gentleman named Jeffery, received in the fray a wound of which he died on the spot.

About two months after this same Jeffery appeared to a gentleman named Milo, and begged him to tell Humbert in whose service he had lost his life, that he was in torment for having assisted in an unjust war, and for not having expiated before his death his sins by penance; that he intreated him to take compassion on him and his father Guichard, who had bequeathed him vast possessions, which he had idly lost, besides one part of which was dishonestly acquired; that in fact Guichard, Humbert's father, had embraced a religious life at Cluny; but that he had had time to satisfy the justice of God for the sins of his past life; that he conjured him then to offer for him and his father the sacrifice of mass, to give alms and obtain the prayers of people of fortune in order to procure them both a speedy deliverance from the troubles they had endured. He added, tell him that if he will not listen to you I shall be obliged to go myself and announce to him what I have just told you.

Milo acquitted himself faithfully of his commission. Humbert was terrified at it, but he did not become the better for it. At all times fearing lest Guichard his father, or Jeffery should come to trouble him, he never dared to stay by himself, and more especially during the night, he always made some of his people be with him to keep him company. One morning as he was lying awake in his bed, he saw Jeffery stand before him, armed as in the day of battle, who shewed him the mortal wound he had received, and which appeared still quite fresh. He reproached him bitterly for the little compassion he shewed towards him and his own father, who was groaning in torments. "Take care," added he, "lest the Almighty should treat you in his wrath, and deny you the mercy that you refuse us; and more especially, take great care to execute the resolution that you have taken to go to war with the Count Armedes; should you do that, you will lose your life and fortune."

He spoke, and Humbert was just going to answer him, when Squire Vichard, Humbert's counsellor, arrived from mass, and the spectre disappeared. From that moment Humbert laboured seriously to comfort his father and Jeffery, and resolved to make the journey to Jerusalem, in order to expiate his sins.

This fact is related by Peter the venerable, abbot of Cluny.

The Ghost of a Young Lady commits several acts of violence.

In the country of Itatans in Peru, a young lady named Catharine, died at the age of sixteen, an untimely death, and guilty of several sacrileges. Her corse immediately after her decease was so infected, that it was obliged to be put in the open air, in order to get rid of the putrid odour that exhaled from it. At that very hour dreadful howlings of dogs were heard; and a horse before exceeding tame, began to prance, kick, tear up the earth with his feet, and afterwards broke from his stable. A young man who was lying in his bed was torn out of it by his arm with violence. A servant received a blow upon the shoulder, of which she carried the marks for several days. All this happened before the corse of Catharine was inhumed. Some time after several inhabitants of the place saw a great quantity of bricks and tiles thrown with a great noise off the house in which she died. The maid-servant of the house was dragged along by her leg, without any one apparently touching her, and that happened in presence of her mistress and ten or twelve other ladies.

The same servant going into a room to take some cloaths, perceived Catharine, who arose up to seize an earthen vessel. The girl fled immediately, but the spectre took the vase, threw it against the wall, and broke it in a thousand pieces. The mistress having ran at the noise, saw a quarter of a brick dashed with violence against the windows. The next day the image of a crucifix affixed to the wall was suddenly torn away, in presence of all the house, and broken in three pieces.

A Young Gentleman troubled by the incantations of a Wizard.—
A fact related by a Clergyman.

On Friday the 1st of May 1705, about five in the evening, Dennis Misanger, a young man eighteen years of age, was attacked with an extraordinary malady, which commenced by a species of lethargy. Every surgical and medicinal aid was given him: he then fell into a species of madness, or convulsions, when he was obliged to be held by five or six persons, fearing lest he should precipitate himself out of the windows, or beat his brains out against the wall. The emetic which was given him, made him cast up a quantity of bile; after which he was tolerably composed for four or five days.

Towards the end of the month of May, he was sent into the country to take the air: he again was taken with another indisposition, so very unusual that it was thought he was bewitched; and what confirmed them in their conjecture, was, that he had never had a fever, nor ever lost his strength in all his illness. They asked him whether he had never had any dealings with any one suspected of sorcery or witchcraft.

He declared that on the 18th of April preceding, as he was riding through the village of Noisy, his horse stopped short in the middle of Feret Street, opposite the chapel, and in despight of all his efforts with the whip and spur, he could not make him go on. A shepherd was at that time leaning against the chapel with a crook in his hand and two black dogs by his side. The man advancing towards him, said: "Sir, I would advise you to return home, for your horse will go no farther." Young Dennis spurring his horse, said to the shepherd: "I do not understand what you say." The shepherd replied in a low tone of voice: "then I will make you." In fact the young man was obliged to alight from his horse, and lead him by the bridle to his father's, who lived in the same village: the shepherd must have then set a spell upon him which commenced on the first of May.

During this illness several masses were said in different places, more especially at St. Maur-des-Fosses, St. Amable, and St. Esprit. Young Dennis was present at some of the masses which were said at St. Maur; but he declared that he should not be cured until Friday 26th of June, on his return from St. Maur. As he was going into the room, having the key in his pocket, he found the shepherd seated in his arm chair, with his crook and two dogs; he was the only one that saw him, no other person in the house perceived him; he said that the man called himself Damis. He saw him during the whole of that day, and all the following night. About six in the evening, being in his usual fits, he fell upon the floor, screaming out that the shepherd was upon him, and crushing him; at that very moment he drew out his knife and cut the face of the shepherd severely in five places, and left the marks perhaps for ever. The patient said to those who were watching him, that he was going to have five or six considerable fainting fits, which would agitate him violently, and begged them to assist him. The thing happened just as he had predicted.

On Friday the 26th of June, Mr. Dennis having gone to mass at St. Maur, told every body that he should be cured on that day. After mass the priest put the stole upon his head, and recited the Evangelist according to St. John. During this prayer the young man saw St. Maur standing up, and the unfortunate shepherd on his left with his face streaming with blood, which issued from the five wounds that he had given him with the knife. The young man instantly shrieked out involuntarily, O miraculous! miraculous! and exclaimed to all around him, he was cured; as he was, in reality.

On the 29th of June, the same Mr. Dennis returned to

Noisy, and amused himself with the diversion of coursing: the day following as he was sporting with his gun among the vines, the shepherd presented himself before him; he struck him with the butt end of his fowling piece; the shepherd exclaimed out, Oh! you have killed me, and fled. The next day he again presented himself to him; threw himself upon his knees, asked his forgiveness, and said; "I am called Damis: it was I who set the spell upon you, which was to continue for a year: through the aid of the masses and prayers that have been said for you, you have been cured in less than two months; but the spell is fallen upon me, and nothing but some miracle will cure me; let me beg of you to pray for my disordered soul."

In consequence of a report being spread abroad, the guards went in pursuit of the shepherd, but he escaped; having destroyed his two dogs and thrown away his crook. On Sunday the 13th of September, he went to Mr. Dennis, and related to him his adventure; that after having been twenty years without approaching the sacrament, God had pardoned him through confessing at Troyes; and that after various refusals, he had at last been admitted to the holy communion. A week after this, Mr. Dennis received a letter from a woman who called herself a relation of the shepherd's, which informed him of his death, and intreated him to order a mass of *requiem* to be said for his departed soul; which was executed.

This fact is related by the reverend father Le Brun.

The ghost of a woman appears to her husband five years after her death to warn him of his future conduct.

ON Tuesday, the 11th of December, 1616, in the street of St. Genevieve; in the suburbs of Paris, a man named Mallebranche, a marker of the game of tennis, between four and five in the morning hearing an uncommon noise, and not knowing who could knock at his door so early, asked who it was: a feeble and incoherent voice replied it was his wife, (who had been dead five years prior to that epoch) who desired to speak to him, and tell him something that concerned him, as well for the safety of his soul as his private conduct. The poor man, greatly astonished, knew not what answer to make, laid silent.

The spectre then resumed with a louder tone, "What, do not you know that I am your wife? I am come to inform you that unless you do penitence, your soul will perish."

As these circumstances are extraordinary, and can very seldom happen except the mind is troubled; the husband did not know what to do for the moment; however, after some interval he heard a voice which spoke to him after the following manner: "You must not be astonished, it is your wife that speaks to you who has been dead five years, three months, and ten days; who informs you that she is yet in torture, from which it is in your power to extricate her, if you have ever loved her; and if you will go to St. Cloud and offer up prayers for her with five candles, for the safety of her soul, you will lighten yourself much."

Whether the astonishment was too great for him, he was unable to ask a question, or even to reply; however, after some contrasts that he had in his soul as a man who is well born, and strives zealously to procure the repose of his wife's soul, he went to St. Cloud, where he put up the offerings that she had recommended to him.

Returning home one evening, and thinking himself at rest through having done what he had been commanded, he heard a knocking at his door, and asking at the same moment who it was, he distinguished some voice which said, that she actually acknowledged that he loved and esteemed her since he had been to St. Cloud, according to her request; but that this was not enough, he must go there a second time, and then she should find repose.

The report of this affair was so noised about the city, that on the Friday following, two capuchin friars were sent for, as virtuous characters, and who think of nothing but the simplicity of life.

They saw, considered and viewed attentively in their minds what this prodigy might be, but having no other certitude of the fact they advised the man not to go again to St. Cloud, if he had no other omens of greater consequence, as the devil might have done it in order to deceive him.

However the marker had his usual visits paid by a knocking at his door, till the Sunday following; wearied out, and pretending not to hear, he distinguished a voice that called out and enquired who was at home.

He would not answer, and made as though he were deaf; but the voice continuing at the door, his wife (being married a second time) cried out, "who is there?"

The voice replied as if it proceeded from a profound cavern, "It is I who wish to speak to my husband; I know very well that you are his present wife, but I have been so before you, and am not concerned on account of his marrying you after my decease; but as to the rest that he has to chastise himself, to acknowledge himself, and more especially to correct his bad habitudes, and to prevent him swearing any more in the name of the sacred and holy God as he usually did; that he may live in comfort with his family and all his neighbours; but more especially that he may not torment his children, or beat his wife, since God has permitted him to have another.

Besides that I have one thing to recommend him; that is before twelfth day which will come very shortly, that he makes a great cake, and assembles all his neighbours to come and receive part of it; and that my share may be left, as I promised all my friends before my death to spend twelfth night with them, but now I am not able, however it is my wish it may be done, and after that I shall be in repose. In fine, let my husband pray for me, and I will pray for him, as I am in great torture."

The Sunday following, we are not certain whether it was by the command of the lord cardinal bishop of Paris, in the evening one of his gentlemen almoners, wished to go and sleep there on purpose to view attentively the affair, and take care there was no imposture.

But lo! as curiosity commonly leads mankind, and more especially the French, to wish to see every kind of novelty, the house was very soon filled with visitors; at the same time they heard nothing, as the voice was silent that very morning (whether on account of the multitude or otherwise) and continued so ever after.

A young gentleman who sold himself to the devil.

A GERMAN gentleman whose name was Michael Lewis, of the family of Boubenhoren, having been sent at an early age by his parents to the duke of Lorraine's court, in order to learn French, lost all his fortune at the game of cards. Reduced to despair, he resolved to give himself up to the devil, provided the evil spirit could or would furnish him with some good money, for he had no doubt but he could furnish him with plenty of bad. As he was occupied with this thought, he saw suddenly a spectre appear before him in the form of a youth about his own age, well dressed and of a noble deportment, who having asked him the cause of his uneasiness, presented to him his hand full of money, and told him to see whether it was good. He told him to come to him on the next day.

Michael returned to his friends, who were still gaming; regained all the money he had lost, and won all that of his companions: he then returned to his demon, who asked him as a recompense three drops of his blood, which he received in the shell of an acorn; then offering to Michael a pen, he told him to write what he should dictate. He dictated several unknown terms, which he ordered to be wrote upon two different pieces of paper; the one of which remained in the custody of the demon, and the other was put into the arm of Michael, in the same place from whence the demon had drawn blood, when the spectre said, "I engage myself to serve you for five years, after which you shall belong to me without reserve."

The youth consented, although with horror, and the demon failed not in appearing to him day and night, under different shapes, and inspiring him with divers novel and entertaining amusements; but always tending to evil. The fatal term of five years approached, when the young gentleman had attained the age of twenty. He went home again to his father's. The demon to whom he had sold himself, inspired him to poison his parents; to set their *chateau* on fire, and to destroy himself. He endeavoured to commit the whole of these crimes; God did not suffer him to succeed; the pistol with which he attempted to shoot himself having missed fire twice; nor did the poison operate upon his parents.

Every day more and more uneasy, he discovered to some of his father's servants the unhappy state in which he existed, and begged of them to procure him some assistance. Seeing him do this, the demon irritated, seized him by the neck and dashed him violently upon the ground. His mother who was of the heresy of suenfeld, and who had persuaded her son to the same principles, finding no assistance against the demon who possest or beset him, was obliged to put him into the hands of some monks of her acquaintance. However he very soon deserted them and fled to Islada, from whence he was accompanied to Molsheim by his brother, canon of Wersbourg, who put him under the care of the president of the society.

The demon at that period redoubled his revengeful efforts, appearing to him under the shape of ferocious animals. One day amongst others, the demon under the form of a wild man and all shaggy, threw upon the ground a note or agreement different from the true one that he had extorted from the youth in order to try under this false appearance to seduce him from the hands of those who kept him, and prevent him making his general confession. In fine, they had so ordered for him to go on the 20th of October 1603, to the chapel of St. Ignatius, and take with him the original agreement he had made with the demon. The young gentleman made a profession there of the catholic and orthodox faith; renounced the demon and received the holy eucharist. Then sending forth the most horrible shrieks, he said that he saw two spectres formed in the shape of goats of an uncommon size, who standing upon their hind legs, held between their claws one of those notes or compacts. But as soon as the name of St. Ignatius was invoked by commencing the exorcisms, the two goats instantly vanished: soon after this almost without pain or leaving the least wound, the agreement started out of his arm and fell at the feet of the exorcist.

Nothing was then wanting but the second compact, which remained in the demon's custody: the exorcisms were recommenced, St. Ignatius was invoked, and mass was promised to be said in honour of the saint. But a few moments had elapsed, when a hideous and horrible made stork appeared, who dropped from his beak the second note upon the altar.

Pope Paul V. gave orders for an enquiry to be made concerning these facts by the deputy commissioners, viz. Mr. Adam, elector of Strasbourg, and George, abbot of Altoft, when a great number of other witnesses who were interrogated judicially, and who affirmed, that the deliverance of this youth was principally due next to the Almighty's power, to the intercession of St. Ignatius.

There is now to be seen in the chapel of St. Ignatius, in the church of the Jesuits, a celebrated inscription, which contains the history of this unfortunate youth.

The Night Mare.

In a certain village of Moravia, a woman having but recently died, furnished with all her sacraments, was interred in the church-yard in the usual manner. Four days after her decease, the inhabitants of the village heard an extraordinary tumult, and saw a spectre which appeared sometimes under the form of a dog, sometimes under that of a human being, not to one person alone but to several, and putting them in violent tortures by pinching their throat and almost strangling them; it penetrated and so disordered them inwardly, that they were taken with violent faintings, and brought almost to the grave.

The spectre attacked even animals: cows have been often found emaciated and half-dead: sometimes it tied them tail to tail. The animals by their horrid bellowing, marked sufficiently the pain they felt. Horses were frequently seen as if overwhelmed with fatigue, dripping with sweat, chiefly heated upon their backs, quite out of breath, covered with foam, as if they had been [on] a long and painful journey. These calamities lasted for several months.

This fact is made mention of in a little work intitled, *Magia Posthuma,* composed by Charles Ferdinand de Schutz, printed at Olmutz in 1706, dedicated to Prince Charles of Lorraine, bishop of Olmutz and Osnaburg.

*The Spirit of a Young Man appearing to a Clergyman under
various awful shapes, and at every visit makes the most
horrid groans.*

In 1726, a curate of the diocese of Constantia, named Bayer,
having been elected to the curacy of Rutheim, was troubled
about a month after by a spectre or evil geni, under the form
of a deformed peasant, miserably dressed, intolerably ugly, of
an insupportable odour, who came knocking at his door in
an insolent manner, and having taken his station by the fire-
side, said, that he had been sent on the part of an officer of
the prince of Constantia, his bishop, on a certain
commission, which he found absolutely false. He then asked
him to eat; meat, bread, and wine was served up. He took
the meat up with his two hands and devoured it, bones and
all, saying; "Look how I eat meat and bones, let me see you
do so likewise?" He then took a goblet and swallowed it
after his wine. After that he asked for another, which he
served the same, and then retired without bidding the curate
one single adieu. The servant who conducted him to the
door, having asked him his name, he replied; "I was born at
Rutsinge, and my name is George Raulin;" which was all a
fiction. As he was going down stairs, he said, threatening the
curate, "I will let you see who I am."

He passed the remainder of the day in the village,
shewing himself to every body. About twelve at night he
went again to the curate's door, exclaiming three times with
a horrible voice; "Mr. Bayer;" and adding, "I will teach you
who I am." In fact, for the space of three years, he went
every day about 4 o'clock in the afternoon, and every night
until break of day.

It appeared under various forms, sometimes under the
shape of a mastiff dog; at other's under that of a lion, or

other formidable animals; sometimes under the form of a man; at others under that of a beautiful young lady while the curate was at table or in bed, seducing him to impudicity; sometimes he made a noise over the whole house like a cooper heading of casks; sometimes one would have thought the whole fabric was falling to the ground. In order to have witnesses to all this the curate sent for the churchwardens, and others of the village, to be witness of the fact. The spectre diffused throughout every place it went an insupportable odour.

At length the curate had recourse to exorcisms, but they were of no effect; and as his being delivered from these vexations was almost despaired of, he was advised towards the expiration of the third year, to furnish himself with a holy branch on Palm Sunday, and with a sword as holy to that effect, and to make use of them against the spectre. He did so once or twice, and since that time he was never molested. This is attested by a capuchin friar, who was witness to most part of the above, the 29th of August 1749.

The Spectre of a Young Lady who was in the habit of visiting her
sweetheart for the space of six months after she died.

AT Tralles in Asia, one Mochates an innkeeper, cohabited with a young lady named Philinnia, the daughter of Demostrates and Charista. After the decease of this unfortunate, she kept coming every night for the space of six months to see her gallant, to drink, to eat, and to sleep with him. One day the nurse of this young lady recognized her as she was sitting by Machates. She ran immediately to inform Charista of it, who after many objections went at length to the inn; but as it was very late, and every body gone to bed, she was unable to satisfy her curiosity. She went again the next morning, when Machates related to her every circumstance; that since a certain time she had visited him every night, and as a proof of what he said, he opened a little box and shewed her a brilliant ring, that Philinnia had given to him, and the veil with which she covered her bosom, that she had left the night preceding.

Charista being no longer able to doubt the veracity of the fact, gave herself up to shrieks and tears; but as she was promised to be informed on the following evening when Philinnia should be there again, she returned home. The daughter appeared at her usual hour, when Machates sent immediately to apprize her parents; for he began to fear lest some other young lady had assumed the dress of Philinnia in order to delude him.

Demostrates and Charista having arrived, recognized their daughter and ran to embrace her; when she exclaimed; "Oh, my beloved parents, why did you envy my happiness by preventing me living yet three days longer with my adored friend, as I did no harm to any one; as it was impossible for me to come here without the permission of the gods, (that is to say of the Demon, since we cannot attribute a miracle like this to God, nor any of his angel spirits) your curiosity will cost me dear enough."—So saying she fell lifeless upon the bed.

Phlegon affranchised by the emperor Adrien, who had held a considerable office in the town, silenced the crowd and prevented a tumult. The day following the people being assembled at the theatre, they agreed to go and visit the tomb in which Philinnia reposed. The departed relics of her family were all found arranged in their proper places, but the corse of Philinnia was not there; nothing was discovered but a diamond ring that had been given to her by Machates, and a golden cup that she had likewise received from him. After this they returned to the residence of Machates, where the young lady's corse was still lying on the ground.

A magician was consulted, who said that it was necessary for her to be interred out of the limits of the city, to appease the furies and terrestrial mercure, to perform funeral obsequies to the manes of the gods, and satisfy Jupiter the hospitaler to Mercury and Mars.—Phlegon adds, speaking to the person to whom he writes, "should you think proper to inform the emperor of it write to me, in order that I may send you one of those who was witness of the above."

A wonderful and horrid Spectre that appeared to John Helias, Sir d'Audiguer's servant, on the 1st of January 1623 in the church of St. Germain. The recital is by Sir d'Audiguer himself.

LAST Sunday being the 1st of January, that having gone to the temple of Notre Dame about four in the afternoon, to speak to the chief penitentiarist concerning the conversion of John Helias my servant, and having seized the moment and resolution to instruct him before he abjured his error in order that he might know why he quitted his heresy and embraced the true religion; I went to pass the remainder of the day with Doctor Saint Foy, who resided very near me. I sent my servant before and retired after him about six o'clock.

On my arrival I called my servant before I went up stairs; he made no reply: I asked if he was not in the stable, no one could inform me. I went up into my room lighted by a *femme de chambre,* and found the two doors shut, the two keys were notwithstanding in the locks. On entering the first room I called my servant a second time, no one answered; on turning myself round I found him in a reclining posture by the fire, with his head leaning against the wall, his eyes and mouth open in full conversation with himself; but with so much loquacity that one word did not wait for another. "I will do no such thing," said he, "it is in vain for you to propose it, I will serve no such master as you, I will surrender, I will surrender."—At first I thought he was seduced and was not inclined to be my servant any longer, hearing him say that he did not wish for such a master, but hearing him keep saying, "I will do no such thing, it is in vain for you to propose it, I will surrender."—I thought he was inebriated and touching him with my foot, I said, arise drunkard. He only lifted up his eyes dejectedly, for though they were open he had them cast mournfully towards the ground, and as to his body he was unable to move it for a considerable time, and recovering from a senseless langour that had deprived him of his speech, he said: "Oh Sir, I am ruined, I am dead; the devil has been just this moment wanting to take me with him." Still I conceived he had only seen this vision in his sleep; but, "No, no," said he, "he has been here twice, the first time I was in the ward-robe with a candle in my hand, when he asked me if I wished to leave him. As I was going up stairs, I called to my remembrance the late Sir Charles, (he went often to the house a few days before his death); and just as I passed the second chamber I recollected the painter, (that was the late Porbus, who died in the house the preceding year), and after that it occurred suddenly to my ideas, what should I do if the devil was to come in order to prevent my being a catholic; no sooner had I said this, but he appeared before me, and so close that there was no room between us for a third." He adds, that he cast his eyes upon him and seeing him as black as he really is, he asked him, "who are you ?" When the devil replied, "I am your master."—"My master," said he, "does not look like you—he wears a white frill and gold lace upon his cloaths;" a pretty servant not to know his master from the devil, but through his frill and tinsel on his cloaths, which could be but a small distinction in regard to his features! but that was his mode of judgment.—"I am not the master whom you serve at present," said the devil, but I am he whom you have served since you came into the world."— My servant then made the sign of the cross, saying, "In the name of the Father, the Son, and Holy Ghost, good Virgin Mary be my aid!"—the spectre disappeared. He said that, seeing him thus black all over, without a frill or collar to his coat, according to his ideas he conceived it an evil spirit. And observe, that being alone and night, in a spacious house and no other person in it but myself who was in another room, he was not frightened without a cause, to see himself in a third room in company with the devil.

The beginning of this discourse made me more attentive to hear the end. In consequence of which, I commanded him to proceed, when he resumed, that having entered the room, shut the doors after him and lighted a fire; he seated himself beside it and took his rosary from his pocket in order to count his beads; but wishing to be less encumbered, he put it in again and reclined his head against the chimney, through which means he saw a burning coal under the grate when that instant a voice exclaimed, "Well! you mean to leave me then?" He said that at first he thought it was me who spoke to him, and that some one had told me that he did not wish to be any longer in my service; "Pardon me Sir," replied he, "who has told you that?"—"I have observed it," said the devil, "as you sometimes go to church."—"Why so," replied my servant; seeing him right before him and recognizing him, "are you still there? I thought you were gone."— "But why?" said the devil, "do you wish to leave me? I am so good a master, you have served me so long, I have a great many others in my service, I can do as much for you; tell me what profession you will be, you shall learn it; if you have no desire to know any you shall go as fine as any lord in Paris; you shall live in any style you wish; stop, there is some money, take as much as you please;" he then stooped down and counted out more money than a hat would hold, earnestly pressing him to take some in the most fascinating and seductive language. "But this is no command of God's," said my servant, "I have nothing to do with you nor your money neither, (he said that he saw no cross,) although I have served you so long, you have badly recompensed me for it ; I now shall take my leave of you and enter the service of my God." So saying, it is very remarkable that he hastened to say as much as possible fearing the devil should overpower him in words, and gain the victory; but what is more, that when the devil saw that he could not tempt him by the abundance of his money, he wanted to seduce him with a part, begging him to take a crown or any thing, representing to him his poverty. "But I will not have any, I will not have any," said he, "God will give me some," with a constancy that marked a great proof of his vocation. "Do you put your trust in God?" said the devil: "all those who serve him are very poor, you will live and die miserable." Thus seeing that nothing could move him, he added twice, "you shall repent for it." The servant said that at first he was terrified at the threat, but comforted by a marvellous assistance from God, he said, "I have done nothing to you, it is impossible for you to hurt me." I have here copied the precise words of their conversation, except another malice which the demon had, seeing that the other would have none of his money, he wanted to get possession of his rosary; he did not call it a rosary, but, "those beads," said he, "that you have in your pocket, let me beg of you to give them to me." Observe his artfulness, he wished him either to receive or give, in order to seduce him by some means or other, and to contract a second time a new alliance. However being still refused that, he begged at least to throw them in the fire before him, representing to him that they were useless bracelets that ladies commonly wore around their arms and necks. Observe in how many forms this Protheus transformed himself to deceive the unfortunate youth, by how many different methods he attacked him. As to myself, I must confess this confirms me greatly in all the points of the catholic religion; still God be thanked, I do not doubt of any; but more particularly as to the virtue of the rosary, or I should not have much devotion now. But mind the frequent repetition of my servant, "it is no command of the Almighty's—I will do no such thing, it is all in vain, I will not have such a master as you, I will surrender, I will surrender, you shall not prevent me;" upon this I entered the room without his knowledge, and when he perceived me first, he thought I had been the devil going to strangle him, or carry him away; for I have still omitted that he persuaded him a long time to go with him, so that at the commencement he took the devil for me, and in the end he took me for the devil.

After he had related to me all this, I asked him whether he could not represent to me the form that the devil had assumed, and if he had not seen any one whom it resembled. He said that he had never seen any thing of the like, and that he had beheld him twice under different forms; the first at the wardrobe, when it seemed as if his shape was smaller, and his features more human, and less deformed than the second, which was in the room, where he appeared to him much more hideous, having the countenance and shape of a great black man without a beard, his teeth similar to the tusks of a wild boar, his nose very large and picked, bent, and turned up again, his nails exceedingly sharp and long, which he had observed whilst he was counting his money. He often said that he wanted to make the sign of the cross, but that he could not lift up his hand.

Since that time having asked him if he had never seen any visions, he told me that when he was in the service of a knight of Malta, whose name was Tallonniere, and returning one evening from Angouleme to Cognac, he saw something black, that presented itself in the road, but was unable to discern it distinctly; and that last summer being one evening at the same house very late, and lying upon his bed, I being in town, something came up to him that he did not see; it told him to get up and follow him down stairs, which he did into the garden; it made him extend himself upon the ground, when he raised up several devils of the most monstrous shapes around him; he said that he was so terrified, and fetched such a dreadful shriek, that another servant that I had ran to his assistance, with the others that were in the house who wanted him to say the *Jesus Maria,* but that he found impossible.

Suffice it now to say what happened to me; for it is still a mark of his predestination. At the end of the siege of Montauban, a great number of valets were dead and several good masters, as well by disease as war. Amongst others I had lost seven, and was left alone with a comrade who had been very ill, and who had only one valet to serve us both. And as I had lost a servant the latter had lost his master. We met each other at a cross way, he coming from Montauban, and I retiring from Picocos to my quarters; and as the one was looking for a master the other for a valet, we were both of us very happy to meet with each other. A few days after, the siege having been raised, I retired to my father's, where I made a sojourn of three months, after an absence of eighteen years. And come next Christmas it is a twelvemonth since I enquired into his religion; he confessed he was a Reformist, and although I did not lose the hope of seeing him abjure it, I could notwithstanding get nothing out of him. I did not wish to seem to press him, but waited till God, by his divine providence, should turn his heart.

Since being in this city, I made him speak to the Jesuits, and to the chief penitentiarist; but in despight of my endeavours, he never could take the resolution till this moment. Thus the devil never attempted to dissuade him from it until he saw he was resolved; and what prevented him forming an earlier resolution, was on account of the minister of Marton, who had instructed him in his heresy: teaching in this city last year, he saw him sometimes unknown to me, and entertained him in the same error in which he had brought him up, telling him always that he should take care not to become a Catholic, although he afterwards became one himself; but that was in order to gain a lawsuit that he had in this country against a priest of St. Savior, after which he made it his business to change his cassock.

But returning to my valet, I will yet say a few words which will mark a very peculiar instance of the providence of God. Being quite young, his father, who is a Surgeon of Marton, frequently chastised him, in order to force him to go to the minister of whom we have just been speaking; however he stole away the more often to go to hear the priests. Some one having given him an *Agnus Dei,* he was found one day by his father, who having corrected him as usual, threw the *Agnus* in the fire. He said that it was about four hours before it was consumed, although his father threw upon it above a dozen little faggots, and that he said to him, "Father, you will make us both be boiled in the same cauldron; chastise me as often as you please, and return me the *Agnus Dei,* or throw me into the fire after it.

Being at Rochelle, they made him eat fish all the week excepting Friday, when they wanted to oblige him to eat meat; and though he was at that time a Hugunot, he would not do it, choosing rather to have nothing but bread, and suffer the rest to deride him, saying, that "he ought to have a pike or a sole bought for him."

I have mentioned this, as it seems to me that the above are as so many marks of an extraordinary vocation, and by so much the more great, as the person was very young; thinking likewise that the Almighty suffered him to see this last vision to confirm him in the desire that he had ingenuously conceived to be converted, as he has been incessantly since that period pressing me for it, instead of which I formerly used to be pressing him; at the time wishing me to strike two blows with one stone, affecting me in my morals as it did him in his religion, or to say rather, in his heresy, and to oblige me to render this true testimony that I owe to the glory of his name, and to the edification of my neighbour.

The spectre of a shepherd that appeared to several persons, when after having called them by their names, they died on that day week ensuing.

A PASTOR of the village of Blow, near the city of Kadam, in Bohemia, appeared some time, and called certain persons, who all died about a week afterwards. The peasants of Blow interred the corse of this pastor and fixed him in the earth with a hedge stake, which they drove through his body.

Finding himself in this situation, he used to laugh at those who had thus treated him, and told them they were very kind to give him a stick in that manner to defend himself against the dogs. That very night he arose and frightened several people, and strangled a great many more, which he had never done till then. They then delivered him to the executioner, who put him into a cart, in order to carry him out of the city and burn him.

The body, although sometime dead, howled like a monster, and moved its feet and hands like unto one living; and when they began to dissect it with a knife a great quantity of blood gushed out. In fine they burnt it, and this execution put an end to the apparitions and infestations of the spectre.

FINIS.

Printed in the United Kingdom
by Lightning Source UK Ltd.
122144UK00002B/1/A